BUTTERFLY DRE[
AND OTHER NEV
FROM UGANDA

CW01090714

Edited with an Introduction by Emma Dawson

Critical, Cultural and Communications Press
Nottingham
2010

Butterfly Dreams and Other New Short Stories from Uganda, edited by Emma Dawson.

World Englishes Literature (Fiction)
General Editor: Emma Dawson

First published in Great Britain by Critical, Cultural and Communications Press, Nottingham, 2010.

Cover design by Andrew Dawson.

Publisher's website: **www.cccpress.co.uk**

ISBN 978-1-905510-30-6 (UK)
ISBN 978-1-60271-027-6 (USA)

First edition.

Printed by Bookbinding Direct, Keele Staffordshire, UK.

CONTENTS

MAP OF UGANDA

General Editor's Preface

This volume belongs to the Fiction series of CCCP's World Englishes Literature imprint. This series focuses on the production of new writing in English, specifically new World Englishes fiction – a term which is defined in the introduction of each publication in the series. Country anthologies of new writing in English feature here, writing which is newly sourced, edited and presented with a critical introduction.

Each country anthology of new writing goes through a sequence of processes. Firstly, a call for short stories is launched electronically through email lists of writers, writing groups, universities and other relevant organisations. Once submissions have been received and read, a journey to the respective country is arranged by the editor in order to meet with the writers who have submitted their work as well as to offer an opportunity for others who have not yet heard of the project to come along and learn about it.

Making the journey to the country in question is paramount and this is what makes the CCCP's country anthologies different from other anthologies of new writing in English. The journey to meet the writers is one that is made in order 'to listen' and not 'to tell'. The World Englishes Literature imprint as a whole explores being beyond the postcolonial, by 'listening' to those who know, who are writing the literature *now*. This stance diverges markedly from anthologies compiled using already published (and recognised) literature, as well as anthologies which are compiled from 'the Western armchair'.

The critical introduction to the country anthologies benefits from this act of 'listening' and, in doing so, aims to present an accurate portrait of the writing emerging from the country in question. The visit to the country also affords the editor an opportunity to research the history of the place and culture, emerging criticism and contemporary literary events, all of which concern themselves with writing in English. All discussions with writers, readers, teachers and other interested parties who contribute to the debate on writing in English are audio-recorded in order for the material to be reproduced in a sensitive and accurate manner.

The final process is a re-opening of the call for submission within a limited timescale. This is conducted because very often, after the editor's visit to the country, writers continue to hear of the project and wish to submit their work. On the editor's return to the UK, the selection of entries is made in consultation with a second editor and reader. Selected writers are paid for their submissions.

The World Englishes Literature Fiction volumes are compilations of short stories which range from 3,000 to 10,000 words in length. The idea motivating such an anthology of short stories is to offer the reader an accessible and manageable 'taste' of a country's contemporary fiction writing in English. The short story also allows a country's writers to explore a variety of contemporary themes and concerns as well as exhibiting the linguistic diversity of the land in question.

Most of the writers presented in the country anthologies will not be 'known' to the Western reader and also possibly not even to many readers in their own countries. This is a basic aim of the series: to promote new, emerging writers, often unknown to the West, writers who have not been 'endorsed' by Western publishing houses, but whose writing tells wonderful new stories in wonderful new ways.

Emma Dawson

Acknowledgments

To Beatrice – thank you for introducing me to 'the Hill' and for waiting with me whilst my favourite orange shoes got a make-over on the pavement of a busy Kampala street – they are still walking!

To all the FEMRITE members at the offices in Kampala, thank you for the reception and the chance to meet and talk with so many of you.

Thank you to all the writers who submitted in order to be considered for this anthology: keep writing, keep being who you are. A special thank you to the writers who feature here for working with me on editorial changes and considerations. I am honoured to have worked with you and to have produced *your* anthology.

E.D.

INTRODUCTION

This introduction will begin by defining the term 'World Englishes' and explain how this relates to 'World Englishes Literature'. It will go on to address the situation in Uganda, offering a brief history of writing in English in the country and the specific context of Anglophone writing, as it is often called. It will cite the major contributors to this movement. The introduction will conclude by outlining the nature of the contributions to this anthology, the writers and the themes that are present in this contemporary collection of new writing.

1. Defining 'World Englishes Literature'

The term 'World Englishes Literature' is inextricably linked to a field of linguistic interest, 'World Englishes'. The term 'World Englishes' is used to encompass the notions of 'new Englishes' and 'New Englishes' (Jenkins 2006: 22-23). According to Jenkins (2006: 22) 'new Englishes' resulted from the first diaspora, and are to be found in the United States, Canada, Australia, New Zealand and South Africa. By contrast, 'New Englishes' (note the upper case 'New') resulted from the second diaspora, and is understood as being the product of situations in which English has been learned as a second language or is spoken as a language within a wider multilingual selection of languages: such scenarios would include, for example, Indian Englishes, Nigerian Englishes, Singaporean or Philippine Englishes. In short, not only is the linguistic production different of 'an English' and 'English as a

Lingua Franca' (ELF), but the cultural, functional and ideological aspects are also at variance between the two.[1]

Jenkins' definition of 'New Englishes' and 'the second diaspora' (2006: 22-23) may have been influenced by the earlier work of Platt *et al.* (1984) who referred to the phenomenon as a 'New English' (note the singular). According to Platt *et al.* the four defining criteria for a 'New English' are as follows:

1. It has developed through an education system. This means that it has been taught as a subject and, in many cases, also used as a medium of instruction in regions where languages other than English were the main languages.
2. It has developed in an area where a native variety of English was *not* the language spoken by most of the population.
3. It is used for a range of functions *among* those who speak or write it in the region where it is used.
4. It has become 'localised' or 'nativised' by adopting some language features of its own, such as sounds, intonation patterns, sentence structures, words and expressions. (Platt *et al.* 1984: 2-3; original emphasis)

Thus Jenkins' notion of 'new Englishes' and 'New Englishes' (which supersedes the work of Platt and colleagues) are included in the understanding of 'World Englishes' for the purposes of this introduction and the imprint of which it is part.

Kachru's (1982) model helps to highlight the extent of the meaning of 'World Englishes', as his model of the Englishes of the world demonstrates that the 'Inner circle' (although it does include the UK) constitutes the 'new Englishes' (that is, the result of the first diaspora, according to Jenkins) while the 'Outer circle' constitutes the 'New Englishes' (that of the second diaspora). Kachru's model also offers a third dimension to the global production of Englishes, namely that of the 'Expanding circle'. In

---

[1] See Tan *et al.* for further discussion on the difference between EFL and the Englishes of the 'Expanding circle' (specifically 2006: 84-94), as well as Kachru and Nelson for discussion on EFL *versus* ESL in an Asian context (2006: 25).

summary, Kachru's model (of Inner, Outer and Expanding circles) can be taken as wholly representational of what is meant here as 'World Englishes' language production.

Kachru's (1982) model of the spread of English around the world remains one of several base models from which we understand the tripartite *linguistic* phenomenon that is 'World Englishes': the Inner, Outer and Expanding circles roughly correspond to the concepts of English as a native language (ENL), English as a second language (ESL) and English as a foreign language (EFL) respectively. The Inner circle includes the United States of America (USA), the United Kingdom (UK), Canada, Australia and New Zealand; the Outer circle includes nations such as India, Kenya, Malaysia and Singapore; and the Expanding circle includes nations such as China, Egypt, Israel and Japan (see Melchers and Shaw 2003, which devotes a detailed chapter to each of the three varieties).

Even in the Inner circle – that is, countries in which English is the native language – other languages may be spoken. In order to demonstrate how these languages are different from the dominant language, I will identify them as 'diaspora community languages' (see Kalra *et al.* 2005 for diverse discussion on notions of 'diaspora and hybridity'). In the United States, Spanish, Italian and Hebrew are spoken (and written) as diaspora community languages. In the United Kingdom, languages such as Hindi, Punjabi, Gujarati, Bengali, Urdu and Jamaican patois are spoken (and often also written). Numerous other languages of diaspora communities settled from first generation to third or fourth generation in Canada, Australia and New Zealand can also be similarly categorised. Moreover, any amalgamation of either a 'diaspora community language' or a language *per se* with the 'English' of an ENL country will therefore produce yet another 'English'. For example, in the UK, British Asian English is categorized by its own lexemes, phonology and grammar, but British Asian English shifts and changes, depending on whether the variety of British Asian English is spoken by people of Pakistani origin or, say, of Indian origin. Equally it differs (in regional accent, grammar and/or lexemes) depending on where in the country the variety is spoken.

In addition, within the 'Inner circle' there are languages which do not fit into the category of being one of Kachru's Inner circle's Englishes (American English, British English, etc.), or one of the 'diaspora community languages' (Hebrew, Punjabi etc.). The languages that do not fit into either of these two categories can be defined as being Indigenous languages, although this term can hold its own semantic problems. For the USA these languages are (American) Indian languages, for the UK they are Scots, Welsh or Gaelic, and in the cases of Australia and New Zealand there are languages of Aboriginal origins. There are many Indigenous languages that I have not mentioned here and this is because I hope that this brief overview of the language situation(s) in the 'Inner circle' has illustrated sufficiently the complexities of Kachru's notion of 'Inner circle'.

In summary, we can see that Kachru's model is helpful in conceiving of the Englishes of the world and accommodates, to an extent, the complex situation of the multi-Englishes of the Inner circle. Can, therefore, this notion simply be transferred to the formation of 'literary' uses of World Englishes? My own answer to this question, perhaps curiously, is no. Indeed, I would wish to dismiss the 'Inner circle' notion, which is undeniably applicable to language use, as unhelpful in explicating World Englishes *literature*. When the *linguistic* voices (of World Englishes speakers) become *literary* voices (of World Englishes writers), it is my own view that, while Kachru's 'Outer' and 'Expanding' circles remain useful concepts for an explanation of what World Englishes literature is, this is not so of the 'Inner' circle: in my definition, that is, World Englishes literature is *never* produced from the Inner circle.

The issues at stake in this argument are not simple questions of geography, spatial proximity to the English 'Standard', or characteristic linguistic properties: it is more how these matters, in a certain combination, produce varied kinds of writing, some of which I would call World Englishes literature, and some of which I would not (although they are all in play). The lines of this debate have long been drawn up in historic theoretical arguments around colonialism and postcolonialism and the conceptual role played in these debates by the voice of the 'subaltern' (Spivak

1988).[2] Likewise, there is often an assumption that writing from the Outer or Expanding circles is always to be explained by the nature of the 'gravitational pull' of the language of the Inner circle. But in my view the multiple features which determine the voice of a World Englishes writer are not defined by the notion of the voice being that of the 'subaltern' – whether geographic, linguistic, cultural, ideological, or all of the foregoing. World Englishes writers are less and less interested in their putative subalternity to a former colonial power and more and more interested in what constitutes, positively, the identity of the culture from within which they write. Similarly, they are less and less likely to worry as to the relation of the English they use to the notionally 'original' English of the Inner circle. I might therefore best encapsulate my definition as follows: *most (but not all) World Englishes literature explores the culture(s) of the country and people from which it is written (these countries belong to Kachru's Outer and Expanding circles); usually the literature employs the English of that place (to a lesser or greater degree); and, moreover, the writer chooses to write in that English over other languages in which she could alternatively write.*

It follows that World Englishes literature is not a synonym for postcolonial literature, although many countries with a history of (for example) British colonialism produce World Englishes literature. The voice of World Englishes literature is not one that necessarily laments postcoloniality or one that wishes for the 'subaltern to speak' (Spivak: 1988). Rather, World Englishes is (as it were) post-postcolonial, and although its writers may remember and even celebrate a defining moment of political independence from a colonising power (as in India in 1947, Nigeria in 1960, Kenya in 1963, or the Philippines in 1946), it also includes a generation of writers who do not.

In short, this anthology, and the imprint of which it is a part,

---

[2] 'Postcolonialism' or 'postcolonial studies' is understood to span many disciplines (history, cultural studies, ethnography), but for our purposes the term refers to its deployment within literary studies. The term will also be used without the (often deployed) hyphen. Boehmer (2005: 3) distinguishes between 'postcolonial' as being pre-Second World War and 'post-colonial' as being post-war. I shall not deal with 'post(-)colonial' notions of literature to the extent that differentiations of such nicety will be required.

invites readers to move beyond the appreciation of Anglophone writers in relation to their colonial past (which is, predominantly, the inflection which has been given to discussion of their work). It does so in the belief that there are many other avenues for discussion and appreciation of this enormous body of writing. I shall suggest some of these alternatives in the further discussion which follows.

2. World Englishes Literature in Uganda

We cannot speak of World Englishes literature production in Uganda without speaking of Makerere University[3] or 'the Hill', as it was often referred to; for anyone who has ever visited Makerere University, and moreover *walked* to Makerere University, 'the Hill' is certainly not in name only. In the 1960s it was not only central to Arts production in Uganda but also more widely recognised as a force in the region of East Africa. In 1962, through that year's conference 'African Writers of English Expression', Makerere University was recognised as the centre of East African cultural development. This metaphoric 'centre', with the publication of *Transition* magazine (founded by Neogy in 1960), acted as a hub for creative Arts to travel out of Uganda and to travel back in, then be distributed to the wider region of East Africa. The student journal *Penpoint* was an instrument in the celebration of Ugandan writing and it was superseded in 1971 by *Dhana*, which 'helped to reflect Makerere's much more Ugandan student population by that date' (Elder 1993: 52).

'The Hill', supported through networks of East African scholars at home and abroad, European expatriates and East African Asians, in Asia and elsewhere, meant that Uganda quickly became acknowledged as the creative centre of East Africa. Then, and ever since, questions of a homogeneous 'East African' culture have abounded. The 1962 conference saw Africans from far and wide attend, and Achebe described the proceedings as 'Pan-

---

[3] For an illuminating account of early 'Makerere' life, from the building's inception in 1939 onwards, see Macpherson (in Breitinger, 2000).

Africanism at its best' (Breitinger 2000: 2). It was, overall, a positive, progressive event which led, amongst other activities, to Achebe and Alan Hill of Heinemann discussing the start of a new publishing series (Ohaeto 1997: 91-94). Ngũgĩ wa Thiong'o published his novels *Weep Not, Child* and *The River Between* in 1964 and 1965 respectively, as an undergraduate at Makerere, in this new 'Heinemann African Writers' Series'. Ngũgĩ had been very keen to attend the 1962 conference and writes of his motivation: 'The main attraction for me was the certain possibility of meeting Chinua Achebe. I had a rough typescript of a novel in progress, *Weep Not, Child*, and I wanted him to read it' (Ngũgĩ 2004 (1981): 5). Conversely, Ngũgĩ exhibits his scepticism about the conference some lines later: 'Yet, despite this exclusion of writers and literature in African languages, no sooner were the introductory preliminaries over than this Conference of "African Writers of English Expression" sat down to the first item on the agenda: "What is African Literature?"' (Ngũgĩ 2004 (1981): 6).

The conference was testament to an exciting time for Arts in Uganda. One of the earliest publishing ventures in the region was The East African Literature Bureau. Elder (1993) tells us that 'The East African Literature Bureau had been founded by the British shortly after World War II to stimulate writing in African languages' (54) and it housed offices in Kampala and in Nairobi. It was dissolved in the late 1970s and replaced by the Kenya Literature Bureau (Elder 1993: 54). The East African Publishing House (EAPH) was founded in Nairobi in 1965 by London-based publisher, André Deutsch. This company existed alongside Longman, Heinemann and Oxford University Press, amongst others with interests in publishing from Africa. The days before Independence meant that many of the foreign publishing houses endorsed an image of Africa that they saw fit, an image of Africa that they *wanted* to uphold; this was often not representative of the countries in Africa they were dealing with, and thus Independence saw a new turn in the publishing of Ugandan and Kenyan writers in particular, as East Africans themselves finally ran publishing houses such as The East African Literature Bureau.

In 1966 Okot p'Bitek's *Song of Lawino* was published in English by The East African Publishing House (EAPH). This publication was seminal in that it brought Acoli, traditional oral literature, to a wider audience. Gikandi (1984) writes of Okot's work: 'What makes Okot's songs so imaginatively domestic, even revolutionary, is their ability to rely on a traditional African form – the Acoli lyric – and turn it into a contemporary forum of debate and discussion' (231). Nazareth (1984) asserts that Okot's *Song of Lawino* was 'the first "poem" to break free from the stranglehold of British writing' (10). In this same year, 1966, Okot p'Bitek became Director of the Uganda Cultural Centre. Makerere attracted scholars from around the world; Paul Theroux, teaching at Makerere in the late 1960s, wrote his novel *Fong and The Indians* (1968), leaving Uganda shortly after its publication. At Makerere Theroux met V.S.Naipaul, a visiting scholar to Makerere at the time. Naipaul's *In A Free State* (1971) is often referred to as his 'Uganda' novel, and centres on political violence and ethnic diversity. Both writers were not left untouched by their 'Uganda years', and the aforementioned narratives are testament to their years spent in a Uganda building up to the chaos of Idi Amin. Theroux was not alone in writing on the East African Asian experience. This was also explored in Bahadur Tejani's work *Day After Tomorrow* (1971), David Rubadiri's *Bride Price* (1967) and Peter Nazareth's work, including most manifestly *In A Brown Mantle* (1972).[4] Both Tejani and Nazareth had their Uganda citizenship taken away from them during the time of Amin (Nazareth 1984: 8).[5] The narratives of these works are described by Jones (2009) as 'potentially redemptive narratives of individual Asian characters set against – and mostly defeated by – a harder, more general, a-historical characterization of an irredeemably close-minded, economically obsessed, ossifying Asian community, starkly lacking a sense of political or social commitment to the new nations of East Africa'

[4] Kiyimba (1998) looks at these works and more, giving a detailed account of Idi Amin's 'fictionalised' self.

[5] See Theroux (1967) for more information on the treatment of Asians in East Africa, although he does make reference in particular to the situation in Kenya.

(34). This controversial point is also raised in Alibhai-Brown's autobiography, *No Place Like Home* (1995: 156, 184).

But the figures of Theroux, Naipaul, and Alibhai-Brown (the last a graduate from Makerere in 1971) fade into an era we now recognise as pre-Amin. The situation at Makerere University and in Uganda as a hub of cultural production changed dramatically under his rule. President Idi Amin Dada was in office from 1971 to 1979. Ugandan society changed physically, with the expulsion of Ugandan Asians and European expatriates. The Arts scene withdrew and leading figures such as Robert Serumagawere were forced into exile, living dangerously at times over the years. Currey (2008) comments: 'Peter Palangyo, Robert Serumaga and John Nagenda, living in and out of the political centres of their rapidly changing countries, all had lives which were a bit too much like plots for novels' (92). Yet such living became commonplace for many. Okot p'Bitek, from late 1967, lived in exile in Kenya (and died there in 1982). Taban lo Liyong joined him in Kenya, where they both taught at University of Nairobi. Peter Nazareth was also exiled. The founder of *Transition*, Rajat Neogy, was stripped of his Ugandan citizenship and forced to emigrate (Elder 1993: 63). In 1984 Nazareth made an illuminating statement on the destruction of the Ugandan literature scene throughout the Amin years: 'a critic of Ugandan literature has first to act as a retriever of the literature: he has to track down the writers and their work and he has to record the existence of the work before beginning to analyse it' (Nazareth, 1984: 8). The Arts scene was hrown into disarray in Uganda for nearly a decade.

Uganda had, pre-Amin, been a passage for cultural exchange, one between East African countries themselves as well as a gateway to a wider Africa and to Europe. Under Amin the gateway was closed and it became almost impossible for the rest of the world to know what was happening culturally and artistically in Ugandan society. Unfortunately the fall of Amin in 1979 did not automatically mean that the Arts scene was able to spring back into life. It had been crippled by the dictatorship, people had fled, had died, and the infrastructure on which Arts-based activity could take place had been destroyed. It took the early part of the 1980s to build up a sense of national cultural interest and production and the late 1980s and early 1990s show a growing interest in this regard.[6] Yet the impact of the Amin era should not be underestimated in terms of how far stretching, longitudinally, it has proven to be. The legacy of Amin's dictatorship was still felt as late as 2000 (three years before the exiled Amin's death in 2003). Writing in 2000, Breitinger states: 'Cultural discourse in Uganda, it appears, is subordinate to the general political discourse and cannot raise itself up to a paramount status within a system of equally ranked discourses' (Breitinger 2000: 6).

It wasn't until the 1980s that publishing started to pick up pace again. In 1988 James Tumusiime founded the Fountain Group, of which Fountain Publishers Ltd. are part. Led by four individuals, it successfully launched the maiden publication *Who's Who in Uganda* in the late eighties. Today it has over 900 authors on its backlist.[7] Another leader in the contemporary publishing scene is FEMRITE. Not only is it a milestone in the development of publishing literature in Uganda, it is also a marker in Ugandan creative movements more broadly. FEMRITE was inaugurated on 3 May 1996 at The National Theatre in Kampala, driven by Mary Karooro Okurut, who 'had her dream set and nothing could deter her from achieving it' (Barungi 2006: 1).[8] Mary gathered a small group together in her office in the Literature Department of Makerere University and from there the group grew in numbers and ambition. FEMRITE is nearing its fifteenth anniversary (in 2011) and in those years the organisation has been responsible for promoting most of Uganda's up-and-coming writers, female and male. It has produced writers such as Regina Amollo, Jackee Budesta Bantanda, Violet Barungi, Susan Kiguli, Beatrice Lamwaka, Beverley Nambozo, Glaydah Namukasa,

---

[6] A landmark in the rebuilding of Ugandan cultural activity is the Ndere Troupe Centre, founded in 1984 by Rwangyezi Stephen. In 2009 it celebrated its twenty-five years of developing music, dance and the cultures of the Ugandan people (see **www.ndere.com**).
[7] Yusuf Serunkuma of Fountain Publishers, in personal email correspondence.
[8] For an informative account of the development of FEMRITE see Barungi, 2006.

Margaret Ntakalimaze, Lillian Tindyebwa, Hilda Twongyeirwe Rutagonya, and Ayeta Wangusa, amongst many others.

Ugandan writing since the late 1990s has certainly taken shape and there are some external influences at play here; the British Council-based writing programme Crossing Borders has helped to foster new African writing to some extent, and Glaydah Namukasa's novel *the deadly ambition* (2006) is one of the works related to the project, published as part of the 'Mallory New African Writing' series. Glaydah Namukasa's short story 'Living Hope' features in this anthology. The annual Caine Prize continues to act as a motivator for new African writers to get their work known, and Uganda has an affinity with The Caine, given that the Ugandan Monica Arac de Nyeko, the author of the 2004 novel *Strange Fruit*, won it in 2007 with her short story 'Jambula Tree' and that the story 'Tropical Fish' by the Ugandan-born author Doreen Baingana was short-listed for the prize in 2005. Although it is inexact to imply that these two writers and the texts cited are 'representative' of contemporary Ugandan fiction in English, it is still worth noting that the texts are (types of) love story. 'Jambula Tree' challenges perceptions of female love, *Strange Fruit* tells of horrific acts of violence towards a woman as, through her husband, she is caught up in conflict, and 'Tropical Fish' is also set in tension with the threat of racism and cruel colonial legacies presenting themselves daily, whilst challenging the often stereotypical European notion of an African woman's love as self-denying and at the extremes of selflessness. The present anthology also showcases several stories of love, told from both male and female perspectives.

The 2000s have seen film adaptations of texts set in East Africa, and in the case of Uganda the film *The Last King of Scotland* (from the novel of the same name by Giles Foden), directed by Kevin Macdonald, was released in 2006. Such adaptations by UK and American-based production teams do raise issues of representation and the 'retelling' of history. This is important given a trend recognised by Musila (2008): 'an interesting trend [in this regard] is the concern with the wars in Northern Uganda and Southern Sudan with particular interest in the plight of child soldiers' (2008: 76). Ahlberg (2009) suggests reading the contemporary Ugandan love story 'by reflecting more generally upon narrative's relation to political turmoil, violence, and conquest' (407).

If the 'golden days' of 'the Hill' were to return, Uganda would once again be able to fully embrace its position as a creative force in the Arts and literary cultures of East Africa. It would not be wrong to suggest that Uganda's literary scene is growing, is finding new directions and new voices; there is certainly no lack of talent or ideas. This is not said lightly, nor patronisingly; the scripts that were submitted for consideration for this anthology demonstrate clearly that the Ugandan literary scene in English is not short of aptitude or creative minds. Writers do, however, continue to face problems of the quotidian which impact upon the desired ease to write and publish as established and up-and-coming artists.

We wait to see where Ugandan Anglophone writing takes us next and yet at the same time, we remember the struggle of the writers during the Amin years, the destruction of the literary scene and most of all, the irretrievable loss of some of Uganda's most celebrated artists.

3. Write Here, Write Now

This collection of short stories stretches itself along the spectrum of love through to sadness, often within the same story. Princess Ikatekit's 'iLove', an email-narrative, explores what it is to love, its disappointments, challenges and its irreversible consequences. 'G' embarks on an explain-all email to David; she wants him to know the truth but the email is not easy to write; the moments from her past are not easy to relive, albeit electronically. In 'Living Hope' Kato risks his life for love. He escapes from prison to get home to his wife and the child that he has never had the chance to see. After several days traversing difficult terrain, chased by guards like an animal, Kato makes it back to his village and finds his neighbour Mzee, who tells him that Kato's wife waited for him till she could wait no more, her wedding is pending... In 'Impenetrable Barriers' David is doing well at medical school but he needs a job. His friend helps him out and gets him some casual work at a clinic, where he meets Kimuli, and love blossoms. As time goes on, Kimuli becomes more impatient to meet David's family – an event David would like at all costs to avoid, knowing that the meeting of his grandmother, mother and Kimuli – will not be a harmonious one.

Jackee Budesta Batanda's '1 4 the Rd …. til 4am' tells the story of Lumu, who is in a bad way since his 'angelic' girlfriend left him for their communication skills lecturer at Makerere University. All he can do is drink it all away with his Bell lager at the local bar, '1 4 the Rd'. He is the last customer and the waitress has got her eye on him; little does he know that his university dealings are not so distant from her own life. This story takes a frank look at love and life and the harsh reality of being 'involved'.

Love (and humour) are in the air in 'The Wedding Ball' by Ulysses Chuka Kibuuka. Two weeks before Mairikiti is due to get married, he and his fiancée are on their way to organise his wife-to-be's wedding dress. Suddenly he is struck by an excruciating pain in his left testis, and he cannot walk. They call his friend and the trio attempt to get to hospital; Mairikiti is in more and more pain. Will they make it in time to save Mairkiti's left testis? Having lost his right testis in early adulthood, it is imperative they save the left one, will they make it in time, will there ever be a wedding ball for the major?

'The Naked Excellencies' is also a funny story; as security is of utmost importance at the meeting of Uganda's Excellencies, at which a strict dress code is maintained. The dress code however, is responsible for everything that happens at the meeting – everything! The title story is a sad and haunting tale of war in Northern Uganda. Lamunu's family hear that she has been found. Taken by the rebels and made to fight in Northern Uganda, Lamunu is scarred physically and emotionally forever. Her family are at loss at what to do with Lamunu on her return, as she is no longer the same girl. They are patient; they wait for her to speak, to express something, anything… but the key lies in the one thing Lamunu is passionate about.

'The Good Samia Man' by Kelvin Odoobo explores living and working in Kampala, returning 'home' to visit family in 'the village'. The narrative takes a sharp look at the urban and the rural, problematising the often conflicting opinions of 'Uganda' in the protagonist's mind. What is it then, to be a 'good Samia man'?

References

Ahlberg, S. (2009). 'Women and war in contemporary love stories from Uganda and Nigeria', in *Comparative Literature Studies* Vol 46, No 2 pp. 407-424.

Alibhai-Brown, Y. (1995). *No Place Like Home*. London: Virago.

Ashcroft, B., G. Griffiths, and H. Tiffin (2006). *The Post-colonial Studies Reader*. London: Routledge.

Barungi, V. (2006). *In Their Own Words*. Kampala: FEMRITE Publications Ltd.

Boehmer, E. (2005). *Colonial and Postcolonial Literature*. Oxford: Oxford University Press.

Breitinger, E. (2000). *Uganda: The Cultural Landscape*. Kampala: Fountain Publishers.

Currey, J. (2008). *Africa Writes Back*. Oxford: James Currey Ltd.

Elder, A. (1993). 'English-Language Fiction From East Afrcia', in Owomoyela, O. (ed) *A History of Twentieth-Century African Literatures*. Lincoln, USA: University of Nebraska Press.

Gikandi (1984). 'The Growth of the East African Novel', in Killam, G.D. (ed) *The Writing of East and Central Africa*. London: Heinemann.

Jones, S. (2009). 'The First South Asian East African Novel: Bahadur Tejani's *Day After Tomorrow*', in *Contemporary South Asia*. Vol 17, No 1, March, pp. 33-46.

Jenkins, J. (2006). *World Englishes*. London: Routledge.

Kachru, Braj B. (1982). *The Other Tongue: English Across Cultures*. Urbana: University of Illinois Press.

Kachru, Y. and C. L. Nelson (2006). *World Englishes In Asian Contexts*. Hong Kong: Hong Kong University Press.

Kalra, V. S., R. Kaur and J. Hutnyk. (2005). *Diaspora and Hybridity*. London: SAGE.

Kiyimba, A. (1998). 'The Ghost of Idi Amin in Ugandan

Literature', in *Research In African Literatures*. Vol 29 pp. 124-138.

Macpherson, M. (2000). 'Makerere: The Place of the Early Sunrise', in Breitinger, E. (ed) *Uganda: The Cultural Landscape*. Kampala: Fountain Publishers.

Melchers, G. and P. Shaw. (2003). *World Englishes*. London: Arnold.

Musila, G. (2008). 'East and Central Africa', in *Journal of Commonwealth Literature*. Vol 43(4), pp. 75-88.

Naipaul, V.S. (1971). *In A Free State*. London: André Deutsch.

Namukasa, G. (2006). *the deadly ambition*. Devon: Mallory Publishing.

Nazareth, P. (1972). *In A Brown Mantle*. Nairobi: East African Literature Bureau.

Nazareth, P. (1984). 'Waiting For Amin: Two Decades of Ugandan Literature', in Killam, G.D. (ed) *The Writing of East and Central Africa*. London: Heinemann

Ohaeto, E. (1997). *Chinua Achebe*. Oxford: James Currey Ltd.

Platt, J., H. Weber and M. L. Ho (1984). *The New Englishes*. London: Routledge and Kegan Paul.

Rubadiri, D. (1967). *Bride Price*. Nairobi: East African Publishing House.

Spivak, G. (1988). 'Can the Subaltern Speak', in C. Nelson and L. Grossberg (eds.), *Marxism and the Interpretation of Culture*. London: Macmillan.

Tan, P. K. W., V. B. Y. Ooi and A. K. L. Chiang (2006). 'World Englishes or English as a Lingua Franca? A view from the perspectives of Non-Anglo Englishes', in R. Rubdy and M. Saraceni (eds.), *English In The World*. London: Continuum

Tejani, B. (1971). *Day After Tomorrow*. Nairobi: East African Literature Bureau.

Theroux, P. (1967). 'Hating The Asians', in *Transition* No 33, Oct-Nov. pp.46-51.

Theroux, P. (1968). *Fong and The Indians*. London: Penguin.

Wa Thiong'o, N. 2004 (1981). *Decolonisation of the Mind*. Nairobi: East African Educational Publishers.

BUTTERFLY DREAMS
Beatrice Lamwaka

Labalpiny read out your name on Mega FM. This was an answer to our daily prayer. We have listened to the programme every day for five years. You and ten other children had been rescued by the soldiers from the rebels in Sudan. For a minute we thought we heard it wrong. We waited as Labalpiny re-read the names. He mentioned Ma's name. Our village, Alokolum. There could not be any other Lamunu but you.

During the last five years, we had become part of the string of parents who listened to Mega FM. Listening and waiting for the names of their loved ones. We sat close to the radio every day. Our hearts thumped every time we heard Lamunu or Alokolum. Without saying words for one hour and each day we sighed after the programme. When the days turned into years, we prayed more often. Your name seems to have disappeared and our chance of seeing you faded. We waited. We bought Eveready batteries to keep the radio going.

Lamunu, we may never tell you this: we buried your *tipu*, spirit, when word went around that you would not come back to us. The neighbours had begun to tell us that you would never return. Bongomin, who returned after four years of abduction, said he saw your dead body bursting in the burning sun. We never believed you were dead. We also didn't want your *tipu* to roam northern Uganda. We didn't want you to come back and haunt us. Ma never believed for one moment that you were gone. It was her strength that kept us hoping that one day you would return. She said she dreamt that butterflies were telling her to keep strong. The night after the dream there were so many butterflies in the house. We thought she was running mad. We thought you had taken her mind with you.

Ma wore *opobo* leaves for three days to let your *tipu* rest. We knew that she did it to make us happy. We advised her to let you rest so that she could move on with her life. She never did. She walked around as if her *tipu* had been buried along with yours. Your *tipu* was buried next to Pa. We didn't want you to loiter in the wilderness in the cold. Ma said you deserved to rest. To rest peacefully in the other world. Then, we heard your name on the radio. And we didn't know what to do. Run away? Unveil your *tipu*? Let you go on without knowing what we had done? We may never find the courage to let you know this. May be one day you will see the grave with your name on it and then the butterflies will give us the right words and strength to tell you.

You were at World Vision, a rehabilitation centre for formerly abducted children. You were being counselled there. You were being taught how to live with us again. Ma cried and laughed at the same time. Yes, you were alive. We couldn't believe at long last our anxiety would come to rest. That night, Ma prayed. We prayed till cockcrow. We were happy. We were happy you were alive. Pa might have turned in his grave. We were happy to know you were alive.

*

You returned home. You were skinny as a cassava stem. Bullet scars on your left arm and right leg. Your feet were cracked and swollen as if you had walked the entire planet. Long scars mapped your once beautiful face. Your eyes had turned the colour of *pilipili* pepper. You caressed your scars as if to tell us what you went through. We did not ask questions. We have heard the stories before from Anena, Aya, Bongomin, Nyeko, Ayat, Lalam, Auma, Ocheng, Otim, Olam, Uma, Ateng, Akwero, Laker, Odong, Lanyero, Ladu, Timi, Kati. We are sure your story is not any different.

When you returned home, Lamunu, we were afraid. We were afraid of you. Afraid of what you had become. Ma borrowed a neighbour's *layibi*. Uncle Ocen bought an egg from the market. You needed to be cleansed. The egg would wash away whatever you did in the bush. Whatever the rebels made you do. We know that you were abducted. You didn't join them and you would never be part of them. You quickly jumped the *layibi*. You stepped on the egg, splashing its egg yolk. You were clean. You didn't ask questions. You did what was asked of you. It's like you knew that you had to do this. Like you knew you would never be clean until you were cleansed. Ma ululated. You were welcomed home. Back home where you belonged.

We watched you silently. In return, you watched us in silence. We gave you food when we thought you were hungry. You gulped down the sweet potatoes and *malakwang* without saying a word. We didn't want to treat you as if you were a stranger but in our hearts, we knew that you were new. We knew that you would never be the same again. We didn't know what to expect of you. We waited to hear you say a word. We wanted to hear your husky voice. Hear you do the loud laugh you did before the rebels snatched you from us. We wanted to tickle you and watch your body move with laughing. But you were silent. You watched us with awe. You had grown now. Your breasts were showing through the blue flowered dress that you wore.

We greeted you. We thanked God when we saw you. You didn't answer our greetings. You looked at us. We saw your eyes glistening. We knew you were happy to be back. We knew you were happy to see us alive.

That night Ma cried in her bed. She whispered your name time and again as if wishing you would at least say Ma. Although she was happy you were back, she never said it. She expected you to say something. Something that would make her believe your spirit was in that body you carried around. We wanted to know whether your *tipu* had been buried with your voice. We had never been taught how to unbury a *tipu*. We only hoped that your real *tipu* was not six feet under.

We wanted to see you alive again. Although you were fifteen then, we wanted to know if you were still interested in becoming a doctor. We wanted to see you smile again. We wanted to see your eyes brighten as your mother gave you water and did the dance that you liked when you were a child. We wanted something that would make us know that you recognised us. We wanted to do our best to make you happy.

Ma never spoke of the butterflies again. We never heard of the butterfly dreams anymore. We wanted the butterflies to come and say something to Ma.

*

We watched you as you studied our new home. Our new home had become something new. We watched the neighbours watch you with disgust. They were not happy you were back. Some of them still clutched the radio waiting for Labalpiny to read their son's name. They waited to hear him call out their names like *lupok cam* call out our names to give us yellow *posho* and beans.

Lamunu, we no longer till our land. Our children no longer know how to hold a hoe. They have forgotten how the ground nut plant looks. Now, our land buries our children. Our gardens grow huts. We now live in a camp. *Lupok cam* call it internally displaced people's camps. From the sky our camp looks like a farm of mushrooms. We have empty huts with empty people whose *tipu* have been buried or have taken a walk.

Look at the huts, Lamunu. This is something that we don't expect you to understand. Something you couldn't recognize. This is something that we don't understand. This is our home, something that we don't know how to explain to you. Something we took refuge in. This is our home that keeps us alive. Keeps us sane. Just huts. Grass and bricks. Just huts to hide our nakedness. When Latim and his neighbours built their huts here, they said Alokolum was safe. Their children will not be abducted. Their wives will not be raped. They will have something to eat. Then so and so built in our gardens all with the same hopes and dreams. Then everybody wanted to build their huts in our land. We couldn't dig anymore. We had no more food. We later learnt our home had been marked in the map of Uganda as a camp.

Don't look at us like that Lamunu. Yes, we now eat yellow *posho*. Yes, yellow *posho* that Ma used to feed Biko, Pa's hunting dog, before the war. We wait for *lupok cam* to provide us with cooking oil and beans, and of course, yellow *posho*. That's all we eat now. Sometimes we don't have enough. Sometimes *lupok cam* don't even come at all. We scramble to get out of the camp to look for something to stop the gnawing feelings in our stomachs. Just a little something. Some wild plants. Some *malakwang kulu*. Some things that our ancestors never ate. Then we found out there were soldiers guarding us. They don't want us to get out of the camp. Why? we asked. They said they don't want rebels to abduct more of us. These days, my dear, they abduct anybody. Anybody who they can force to stand and be shot in the battlefield.

We asked the soldiers, where were you when Lamunu was abducted. Where were you when the rebels came and took our young ones? Where did you go to when the rebels came and raped our women as we watched? They told us they had not been paid. Sod off! we tell them. Let us go to look for food. Then they came with their sticks to beat us as if we were school children.

*

You spoke in your dreams. You turned and tossed in your mud bed. We held your hands. You were like a woman in labour. You spoke of ghosts. You spoke of rebels chasing you in Adilang because you tried to escape. You spoke of Akello, your friend, who they made you and your team beat to death because she tried to escape. You said you didn't want to kill her. You said you remembered the commandment 'thou shall not kill'. You said you didn't want to participate. You didn't want to hurt anybody. You said you saw Akello covered with sticks. You saw the blood in her mouth. You watched as the older rebels checked to confirm that she was dead. You were nauseated. You tried to vomit but there was nothing to let out. The last meal, raw cassava and boiled chicken, which you had looted from a camp, had already been digested.

We listened to you. We wanted to feel your pain. We wanted to know what you knew. We squeezed your hand. We wanted you to let out what you had been holding onto. You let us squeeze your hand. You didn't wince when blood flowed. We never could drain all your pain away.

*

Today, we watched you get drenched in the rain. You stood there still as the rainfall poured on you. You were not disturbed by the loud thunderstorm. We made space for you in the hut. Waited for you with warm clothes. We thought you were letting out something. We didn't interrupt you.

As the rain became a drizzle, you entered the hut. You bypassed Ma with the warm clothes in her hands. You sat with your wet clothes on. We noticed that it was the time of the month for you. You let the rain wash the blood away. You let us watch the blood streak down your leg. You didn't see the tears rolling down your mother's face.

Later that day, we listened to you curse under your breath. We watched you tremble when you heard the government fighting planes flying over Katikati. We knew that you were worried about the people you left behind. We knew that you knew what would go on when the planes went after the rebels. We didn't ask you for stories. We have heard the stories from Anena, Aya, Bongomin, Nyeko, Ayat, Lalam, Auma, Ocheng, Otim, Olam, Uma, Ateng, Akwero, Laker, Odong, Lanyero, Ladu, Timi, Kati.

*

Lamunu, we remember as if it were yesterday when the rebels came to our home. That night was the night we knew that there would be many more nights like that one. We heard the butts of the guns hitting people's heads. We heard the screams. We heard the rebels demanding our children from our own homes. We were helpless.

You were still dazed with sleep. One rebel not much older than you grabbed you by the hands. You were only wearing a t-shirt. Ma grabbed a skirt for you to wear. You went out of the house with it still in your hand.

Ma's pleas and cries were only answered with the butts of guns on her head. She asked them to take her instead. But the rebels demanded medicine. They wanted the medicine she brought from the government hospital in town. Lamunu, Ma would never have let you go. You were only eleven. Reading for your Primary Leaving Exams. You always wanted to be a doctor. You said you wanted to do what Ma was doing, not as a nurse, but as a doctor.

We later learnt that they went house to house in Katikati as well, taking all boys and girls around your age with them. They said that the rebels would train the children to fight. Train them to lure other children. Join the big war to save the Acholi. Oust the government. Overthrow Museveni's government. We didn't know what that meant. We didn't want to ask anyone. What we knew was that we didn't want our children to get involved in that war.

*

We watched as you always prepared to go to school like it was a special ritual. Brushing your teeth and then taking a bath. You carefully splashed the water from the *galaya* onto your slender body. You didn't eat the breakfast that Ma made for you. You packed it in your school bag so that you wouldn't be late for school. We admired you for that. Even when the war started and many children were waylaid, you managed to get there. You cursed the teachers and called them cowards when you didn't find any children or teachers. Days after a heavy fight between the rebels and soldiers you continued to go to school. You never gave up even when you didn't find anybody there.

You said that the war only affected the education of the children in the north. The rest of the children in Uganda studied. And the exams were all the same. You went to school when everyone was hiding in the bush. Ma begged you not to go. Children were waylaid by rebels on their way to school she pleaded. You always managed to get to school. Found an empty class. Disappointed, you would come home. Ma later became your teacher. Ma taught you about reproduction even if she knew she shouldn't say such words to her daughter. You were eager to learn. Pa wanted to teach you too, even though he didn't know how to read and write.

*

Lamunu, we don't know how to tell you that Pa is no longer with us. You may have noticed that he is not around. We don't know with which mouth to tell you that he was cut to pieces by those who you were fighting for. He was found in a garden he rented in Lalogi. He said he could no depend on *Lupok cam* to provide him and his family with food. You know your father. He was a proud man. He believed that a strong man should show his strength by the amount of food he had in his granary. Before the war, there was a lot of food in the granary. The neighbours were jealous of that. He dug like a tractor. His cows were the best in Alokolum. Everybody wanted to buy milk from him. Even the lazy Lutukamoi, he tried to dig night and day but couldn't get done half of what your father could achieve.

The rebels found him digging and asked him what he was doing since everybody was supposed to be in a camp. He said a man has to provide for his family. They mocked him and told him to join them to fight if he was strong man. He said he would not join them because he did not start the war they were fighting. Ten young men beat him up with whatever they could find. They later cut his body into pieces. Lamunu, we did not eat meat after we buried your father and we have not eaten meat since then…. We could never understand why another human being could humiliate another, even in their death.

Each day we pray that we get the strength to tell you. And one day when the war ends, you will tell us your story. And we will tell you our stories.

*

We learnt from the neighbours that you went to school. You asked the headmaster to register you as a primary six pupil. We didn't know that you could talk. We were happy that you said something, even though it wasn't to us. The headmaster looked at your skinny body. You told him you wanted to become a doctor. He asked you whether you could pay. You didn't answer that. You knew that we didn't even have a coin to put food on the table. You said you didn't care and that all you wanted to do was to study. You said you could pay when you were finished with your education.

You entered a primary four class. The pupils watched you silently. They thought you were a mad girl. They muffled their screams, worried that you would hit them or something. They knew that the war had brought something that they don't understand. They wanted to survive, so whatever didn't kill them they would watch to try to find a way.

Ma ran to school when she heard that you were there and argued with the headmaster. She wondered why you didn't tell her anything. She wanted to help you. She wanted you to talk to her but she didn't want to push you as well. She loved you though she could not say it.

*

Ma spoke to the headmaster of Lacor Primary school. The headmaster agreed to let Ma pay your school fees in instalments. She said that she is happy that you still want to go to school.

You said *apwoyo*. You said thank you to Ma. That's the first word we have heard you say. We're happy to hear you say something. We hope that you will be able to say a lot more. Tell us more than Anena, Aya, Bongomin, Nyeko, Ayat, Lalam, Auma, Ocheng, Otim, Olam, Uma, Ateng, Akwero, Laker, Odong, Lanyero, Ladu, Timi…. Most of all, we want to hear your voice.

*

You look very beautiful in your new uniform. The headmaster of Lacor Primary School for formerly abducted children has donated the uniform to you. Ma says that you will get special treatment. Most of the children are like you. They too have killed, tortured other children. They too fought in a war that they didn't understand. The teachers will treat you well, Ma says. They have had special training.

You are very happy. We can see you have woken up early. You

have packed your bag with your new books. You have written your name neatly written on the books.

We know that your dreams will come true. You will be a doctor some day. Do the work that Ma does but wearing a white coat.

There are tears in Ma's eyes. You look the other way. We know that you know they are tears of happiness.

IMPENETRABLE BARRIERS
Violet Barungi

As David sat dejectedly staring out of the window at the morning sunshine, his heart uncomforted by the promise of a lovely day, his roommate Jimmy Ngabirano walked in.

'Hi,' Jimmy said cheerfully. Then he noticed the forlorn look on the other's face. 'Why so low? You're not worrying about those supps, are you? You're lucky you got away with only two. I have three and I know of some guys who have been advised to re-channel their interests in other fields,' he added in his flippant manner.

David secretly admired and envied the lank-lean, dark-skinned Jimmy, his worldly view to life and especially his easy-going manner. Nothing ever seemed to ruffle his good humour. He occasionally disappeared on a drinking binge and came staggering back into the room in the early hours, and yet he always recovered with surprising alacrity. With a rueful smile and a philosophical shrug, he'd disappear down the corridor to the shower room and emerge a few minutes later a new man. He was a very intriguing person.

'Oh that,' David said, dismissing the subject of supplementary exams as a trifle. 'I'm not worried about that.'

'What's biting you then? Not bad news from home, I hope?'

'No,' David answered reticently, but after a brief pause, he thought what the hell, and proceeded to confide his worry. 'The fact of the matter, Jimmy, is that I need a job during the vac to earn a few bucks to survive.'

'How have you managed before?' Jimmy asked, giving David scanty attention as he rummaged through the wardrobe for something to wear. Jimmy was quite fond of David, but as he liked to act like a loner, he could not afford to show his feelings. Interestingly, right from his first encounter with David, he had felt an instinctive liking for the simple village lad.

'I used to go home for the breaks but now I've got to stick around for the remedial tests and well, things are not frightfully easy at home,' he added, attempting a nonchalant shrug. 'I might as well spend the whole vac here if I can find employment.'

'You're serious about getting a job, aren't you?'

'Yes, I am.'

'Well, let's see. What you have to offer: third year medic, what are you qualified to do?'

'Nothing I guess. But I'm prepared to try my hand at anything, short of cleaning toilets and pushing wheel barrows in the market.'

'Tsk, tsk. What would your friends say?' Jimmy teased, shaking his head. David narrowed his eyes, offended at the reference. His previous roommates had been different from Jimmy. David had first met them when they had all been freshmen, eager to discover the world. He had at first baulked at their enthusiasm to live it up, reminding himself that he was at the university for a purpose, and that purpose did not include drinking, exploring the city's night spots and taking out girls. But his new-found friends had kept up the pressure until he gave in and started to relax. By the time he went into his third year, he had a reputation as a hard-drinker and his academic performance had consequently been affected.

However, his new roommate, Jimmy, was not the chummy type. He had a detached manner which enabled David to rethink his priorities and, more importantly, to keep the door to his skeleton cupboard firmly closed.

'Okay,' Jimmy went on, 'I'll see what I can do.'

'O, thank you.'

'Hold it. *Akutwaara ekiro* and so on… I haven't delivered yet,' Jimmy raised his hands. 'Besides, you might not like the job I'm going to suggest. But it falls within our line of interest.'

'A hospital orderly?'

'With the appalling rate of unemployment? You should be so

lucky. But I have a brother who runs a clinic in town where I have sometimes worked.'

'But isn't that illegal?' David asked uncertainly. He saw himself botching abortions and being hauled before the law to answer charges of illegal practice, murder and whatnot.

Reading his thoughts, Jimmy said with a smile, 'Don't overrate yourself pal. All you'll be required to do is to run errands of sorts. Can you handle that?'

'Sure,' David assured him enthusiastically. 'I'm grateful, Jimmy'.

*

David reported to Dr Sewabirya at the City Centre Clinic with a note from Jimmy. The job at the clinic was not heavy and occupied him only during the daytime. He used the evening time to study but, quite often, found himself at a loose end since the crowd had left campus for the long vac.

Eventually he struck up a friendship at the clinic with a girl called Kimuli, which showed every promise of growing into something more serious. Kimuli was as beautiful as the flower she was named after; intelligent and compassionate. David watched how she handled patients daily at the clinic and was impressed. This is the girl made for me, he said to himself. But although he loved her as he had never loved any other girl, the problem of who he was and where he came from posed a challenge to his relationship with her and in truth, to all the other relationships he had tried to make before. Kimuli tried to make him open up a little and talk about his background without success.

'You don't love me, David, do you?' she complained one day.

'Of course I do, Kim. Where I come from has nothing to do with how I feel about you,' David assured her. 'You have my heart which is the centre of my being. What more do you want?'

'The real you.'

'This is the real me: David Buhamiro, aged 24, third year medical student. I'll even give you a life-size portrait of myself you can study at your own leisure,' David told her, trying to speak lightly, yet inside he was churning with cheerless emotions. His nemesis was catching up with him at last.

'This is not a joking matter, David,' Kimuli rebuked him, her pretty broad face creased with a frown. 'I love you so much that I want to know everything about you. I want to know your background so that I can picture you as a baby, a toddler, a schoolboy and so on. I want to know something about my rival, the woman who held you in her arms and raised you to be the man you are now.'

'Precious, you don't want to know my dismal background, believe me. Try to imagine I have no background; the man from nowhere.'

Try as he could, David could not erase his origins the memories of which still made him flinch with pain. He was still the kid other kids made fun of; tortured, and made to feel like a freak of nature. His dreams were still dominated with sad images of the friendless, lonely kid other kids in Kagadi village never invited to play games with. He was still that kid, and he could never run away from him, whatever changes the passage of time had inflicted. His past was always there, at the back of his mind; compelling him to imagine everybody viewed him against his background and found him needy. This inevitably interfered with his growth of self-knowledge, eroding his confidence to appreciate the real person he really was, or could be, given the chance; a young man with a lot of potential to make a difference in his world, if only he could throw off the shackles binding him to his ignominious past.

*

David grew up in an extremely poverty-stricken and miserable home that even by village standards was at the absolute limit. He had no father and lived with his mother and grandmother in a tumbledown mud and wattle structure that passed for a house. The three of them were regarded as social outcasts because of their utter poverty. From what David gathered, his father was not dead but had abandoned him and his mother under unclear circumstances. According to his grandmother, though, he was a good-for-nothing son of a witch, and one she would sooner spit at than shake hands with, as she colourfully put it.

Lakeri, David's grandmother, was a harsh, cantankerous old woman who never saw any good in anyone, especially her absentee son-in-law. She was the mistress in the home and ruled David with the cane. How miserable she made him and how he hated the old woman and longed to escape from the dreadful home!

His mother, on the other hand, was quiet and gentle and doted on him. But in spite of this, she was the fly that soured his milk, responsible for blighting his young existence more than his battle-axe of a grandmother. His mother did not set out to intentionally heap more misery on his already bent back; it was the curse she carried that impacted on his life as her son.

Sometime before David was born, his mother was badly burnt in a fire and hideously disfigured. The right side of her face was completely destroyed from the crown to the neck, leaving a shrivelled, ugly expanse. To keep the scarred part hidden from view, Erina went about veiled in tattered black pieces of cloth from head to waist that lent her a sinister appearance and earned her the reputation of the village witch. The children at school bullied and tormented David so much on account of her that, quite often, he fervently wished he were dead. But he bore it all; he hated his mother and grandmother vigorously and he looked to the day he would turn his back on them for good and on the wretched old place.

The question of how his mother had come by those awful scars occupied his thoughts a lot, but whenever he dared to ask his grandmother, all he got were a volley of insults and scolding. Why couldn't he have a normal family like other kids with a father, mother, brothers and sisters? He hated the poverty; the ugliness and the eccentricity of his existence that made him feel like a crow among the beautifully crested cranes. As a result of these circumstances, David became completely introverted and avoided making close friends with other kids. He didn't have a single friend at school or in the village. Friends exchanged secrets; friends visited each other; but he was ashamed to take anybody to his home. Besides, none of the other boys would be seen dead in the company of the 'son of a witch'.

One day, David came home from school feeling particularly miserable and desperate. His tormentors had taken advantage of the class teacher's absence to amuse themselves at his expense. They had started by drawing pictures of an obnoxious looking creature on the blackboard. It seemed that almost half the class took turns at distorting the image, vying with one another as to who could make it look scarier. When they were done, the representation looked spookier than *orukooko*, the ogre used to scare children into behaving properly.

David felt outraged at the slanderous lies about his mother. He wished he had the strength of the biblical David so that he could knock down the snooty imbeciles with one sweep of his hand or that he possessed magical powers to make himself disappear in a puff of smoke! As it was, he could only cringe and pretend to ignore the giggles and the sly glances. He knew they wanted him to cry so that they could call him mucus licker and laugh at him, but he clenched his jaw and silently prayed to God to strike the entire lot dumb.

'Does your mother stir your porridge with the hand of a dead body she has exhumed from the grave? And I'm naming no names but when they talk of a bent top, there's no need to mention a machete,' said one particularly obnoxious boy called Bigirwa, standing in front of the class.

This purported joke was received with bursts of laughter and chanting of made-up jingles they imagined his mother recited on her ill-intentioned nocturnal wanderings. In the ensuing uproar of frolicking and prancing around the room, David unobtrusively stole away, preferring six hard thrashes from the teacher's cane on his bottom the next day to the merciless taunting.

He walked fast, not because he was eager to get home but because he could not hold his tears back much longer. He needed to get to his secret place fast enough to release the burning tears from behind his eyelids. The place was near his home but was hidden from view by clamps of *ekizibwe* grass which grew luxuriously tall and thick. David often ran there for refuge when he felt the world closing in on him. Here he could spill out his guts without the fear of being laughed at. Here there was no one to tell him that real men don't cry, as his grandmother never stopped hammering or to call him pant-wetter as his schoolmates often did. Here he felt invisible from the world. Here he felt his bruised soul soothed and healed. Here he felt safe and in harmony with his surroundings and wished he could stay forever.

When he got home that evening, he found his grandmother and mother seated on straw mats under the mango tree in the backyard, sipping brown porridge from plastic cups.

The giant mango tree was like an extension of the main house. It was here that most of the meals were eaten, the few visitors who dropped by were received and his grandmother's aching old bones rested after a day's work in the gardens. She would lie down, sheltered from the glare of the afternoon sun by the bowed heavy branches of the tree and doze until the sharp evening breeze woke her up.

At night, when it was balmy and clear, with the sky lit by a full moon and a host of bright stars, his mother and grandmother sat talking late into the night. What they talked about, David did not know and had no desire to know. He would remove himself a little way off to the veranda to do his homework under the benign gaze of the woman in the moon who seemed to say to him, 'Dream on and one day you'll join me in my pearly abode'.

That evening, David stopped at the corner of the house, half hidden by the wall. With 'son of a witch' chants still ringing in his ears, he felt an overwhelming desire to know the story behind his mother's deformity.

As long as he could remember, he had always found his mother's unsightly face repulsive. He always endeavoured as much as possible not to look at it, which was easy since she kept it hidden under wraps most of the time. It was only at times like this, when the two women were alone, that Lakeri encouraged her daughter to relax and uncover her face so that the cool air could caress it.

As David studied his mother now, he realised how easy it was for people who did not know her to mistake her for a witch, especially when seen in the dark. He wondered how she had come by those scars. Why did his grandmother become so grouchy whenever he attempted to find out? Could she have actually been a night-dancer who people had attempted to burn after catching her in the act? This was quite believable, given that his grandmother never wanted to mention the subject. To that, add that the family was not a native of Kagadi but had migrated there when David was a baby and... Why had they run away from their own village? What about his father; why had he abandoned them? Was it because he had discovered that he had married a night-dancer? All these mysteries teased David's brain and made him reel under their weight.

'What are you standing there gawking at?' Spotting David, his grandmother yelled at him. 'Have we grown horns that you cannot take your stupid eyes off? Put your books away and get on with your chores. Your porridge is on the fire and you can get it yourself. Nobody is paid to wait on you.'

'I don't want it,' David mumbled sullenly and went in the house.

'Suit yourself, it's your stomach that will go empty. But don't imagine that will excuse you from attending to your duties. So hurry, or Judgement Day will be here before you're started!' she admonished. The cruel old woman, David thought resentfully.

'Perhaps he's not feeling well,' his mother said tentatively, starting to rise to follow him. 'He doesn't look himself today, and did you notice the way he was gazing at me?' she added, putting on her shroud and drawing it about her more securely.

'You're a fool, Erina, and always have been,' her mother castigated harshly. She was a sharp old woman and it had not escaped her attention that David was ashamed of his mother, the ingrate.

'He might have something on his mind that's bothering him,' Erina persisted, making excuses for her son.

'That rascal has nothing on his mind, if he has a mind. Sit yourself down and stop flapping like a hen about to lay an egg.' Erina complied.

Lakeri took one belligerent sip from her cup and banged it down, preparatory to further verbal attack. 'Erina, when are you going to tell that useless son of yours how you came by those scars? If you're too timid to do it, I'll tell him myself and we shall see whether he still thinks that you look revolting.'

'Please don't, Mother,' Erina implored, her good eye blinking ominously. 'He's too young, and the knowledge might give him a guilty conscience.'

'A conscience, guilty or otherwise, is what he needs to show some gratitude for some of the sacrifices made for him. When, according to you, will he be old enough to handle the truth, to know that his father was a good-for-nothing rogue who abandoned him in a burning house? When will he be able to know that you sacrificed your young life so that he could live? This is the right time, I tell you, when he's young enough to adjust to the truth. I know you think I'm too rough on him but I love him as much as you do. However, there's too much of his father's blood in him that must not be allowed to ruin him. Give and take is an age-old truth he cannot learn early enough, I say.'

'I'll tell him when the time is appropriate,' Erina stated adamantly. Her mother was a tough, overbearing woman and very often bullied her into doing things her way. But on the issue of her son, Erina could also be firm and uncompromising.

'This is the time, I tell you,' the old woman persisted with the obstinacy of somebody used to having her own way. 'I'll speak to him myself.'

'Don't, Mother, or I swear I'll do something drastic. I'll kill myself, I swear, I will,' Erina declared wildly and her mother knew this was no idle threat. Sometimes Lakeri wondered whether her daughter would not be better off six feet under the ground than above it. Deserted by that no good husband of hers on the threshold of her life, charred almost to cinders, her beauty marred forever, living a life that even a flea-infested dog did not deserve, scurrying about like a thief and condemned to a cold bed for the rest of life, her children trapped inside her; where is the fairness, oh God, where is justice in all this, she cried inwardly. She felt overwhelmed by her own emotions and, as usual, took refuge in being more severe with David as if she held him responsible for all that had happened to his mother. 'Where's that cursed boy?' she grumbled, blinking back her tears and getting up to stomp noisily toward the house. 'Shirking as usual, are you?' she screamed at him.

David had just finished folding his uniform neatly and placed it under his pillow as he did everyday to keep it looking neat when he heard the quarrelsome voice. He sighed and went outside.

His duties included collecting water from the communal well, sweeping the compound, cleaning the chicken and goats' house and tethering the goats in the bush in the morning and bringing them back home in the evening. According to his grandmother, all that slogging was meant to mould him into a real and responsible man, unlike his vagabond of a father.

He was just getting started on the compound when his mother sidled up to him and whispered, 'Are you all right?' Why does she creep about like that, David thought irritated. No wonder they call her a witch! 'Leave me alone,' he growled, without looking at her.

Erina watched him helplessly, her heart heavy with sadness before she turned and went back to her world of shadows.

*

David was just untying Kireju, a spirited he-goat which never failed to challenge him to a brisk trot round in circles as soon as he released it when he heard a commotion in the vicinity of his home. Pulling the rebellious goat by its rope behind him, the other four had already found their way home, David hastened along, wondering what could be the matter. Neighbours rarely called on them, and if it were not for his grandmother's nosy nature, they would be no better than people living on an island in the middle of Lake Victoria.

As he emerged from the banana plantation which skirted the small homestead, he saw his mother cowering behind the small kitchen, clutching pieces of a broken water pot, her face full of terror. His heart beating fast, he let go of the goat and advanced forward in search of the source of the uproar. As he rounded the corner of the house, an object, which he later identified as a big pebble, zoomed past him, missing his head by a small fraction. Crouching low and clinging to the wall for support, he peered across the front yard and saw his grandmother, her skirt hitched up, wagging a stout stick towards some retreating small figures in the Kagadi Primary School uniform.

'Show your ugly faces here again, you murderous twerps, and

I'll thrash you to a pulp,' she yelled at them. 'I'll report you to your parents, in fact, I'll report you to the headmaster of your school,' she spluttered further, foaming at the mouth with fury, but the culprits were already out of hearing range. But not before David had ascertained that it was Bigirwa, the goon himself and his stooges, who had been making his school life hell.'

His grandmother turned back to the house, still breathing fire, which prompted David to take cover immediately lest he took the brunt of her pent-up rage. 'The swines, the wretches!' she puffed and ranted, her eyes red and protruding. 'I'll get them if it takes me a hundred years to do it.'

'Mama please, don't get yourself worked up,' Erina pleaded, standing up and dropping the pieces of clay with a clutter.

'Mama please,' the old woman mimicked disparagingly. 'Why shouldn't I get worked up when those little monsters almost killed you? Why didn't you throw that pot at them and let them have a taste of their own medicine? How long are you going to cringe away from injustices done to you? Do you think I'll always be here to fight your battles? But let me tell you, had I been here a minute earlier, those twits would have left here on their bellies or my name is not Lakeri Nyambogo,' she swore.

Then she spotted David peering at her from behind a stout banana stem and pointing her finger at him, she snarled. 'And you good-for-nothing son of a fiend, don't stand there goggling like an owl while your mother bleeds to death. Go and bring water and herbs to staunch the blood'.

David had not seen his mother's bleeding foot, which must have been cut by the water pot as it fell from her head and broke. He felt something heavy squeezing at his heart and, heedless of his grandmother's vituperations, stood still, overcome by feelings of pity and tenderness for his mother. He wished he was big enough to take on those hooligans and avenge himself for all the suffering they made him endure. Two big tears rolling down his face doused his grandmother's rage.

He did not sleep that night. He kept thinking about the incident and wondering why people hated him and his mother so much. Was it a crime to be poor or a cripple? And he then thought what it would be like for him at school the following morning and cringed with dread. His stomach churned with fear at the thought of facing those horrible kids. After dying a thousand deaths at the thought, he knew that he could not go to school the next day or ever again. He carefully planned how he could play truant without his grandmother getting wind of it.

The following morning, he got up as the cock raised itself on its toes to crow for a second time, which was long before his grandmother would shuffle to the corner of the room the three shared to administer her wake-up cup of cold water over him. He went to the well, tethered the goats and put on his uniform as if he was going to school. His mother offered him a plate of cold sweet potatoes left over from the previous evening meal, which he rudely rejected. He was about to depart when his grandmother, in her Sunday best of a voluminous gaudy garment, appeared at his side and announced that she was accompanying him to school. David stared open-mouthed, convinced that by some supernatural powers that only she possessed, she had divined his plot of evading school and was determined to thwart it.

'Bu…buuut, Kaaka…' he stuttered, cringing at the idea. His grandmother escorting him to school after the previous evening's incident would be the last nail in his coffin. His life would not be worth a dog's ear after that. His enemies would chew him alive and spit him out.

'Close your mouth if you don't want all the flies in Kagadi to find a home in that pot belly of yours. The heavens will not come crashing down because an old woman has escorted you to school. So shut up and follow me,' she commanded and David had no choice but to obey.

At school, his grandmother headed straight for the headmaster's office. She was tall and straight-backed, and the furrows and etchings on her aged face made her look so fierce that the perpetrators of the previous day's ugly incident could not help but quake with fear on sighting her.

After narrating the disgraceful and outrageous conduct of pupils of Kagadi Primary School to the head teacher, David's grandmother called for them to be severely punished. 'They are a disgrace to the school and a shame to their parents. An innocent woman was almost killed, my property destroyed and my grandson terrorised,' she stated, her beady eye fixed challengingly on him.

'Can you identify these boys, David?' the headmaster asked. David shifted from one leg to the other, quaking inside.

'David!' his grandmother barked and that was it. He revealed the names of all the boys he saw fleeing from his home and all the other tormentors in class. His life was in God's hands. But after the miscreants had been severely punished and their parents informed, David was left alone most of the time to pursue his studies in peace.

While David was in P6, calamity struck his home. His grandmother, the crutch of the family, died, leaving him and his mother, two helpless beings, to fend for themselves in a hostile world. As far as David could remember, his grandmother had always been the greatest influence in his life. Now she was gone. It was like waking up one morning to find the roof that had sheltered you from rain, the menace of darkness and other unfriendly elements, gone. He could not contemplate a life without her. Who would plan for the future, make important decisions, scold and censure, grumble, regulate and direct his every move? He felt overcome with grief at losing her in spite of her bad temper and meanness.

'How are we going to manage?' he asked his mother as he unashamedly wept in his hands.

'Life goes on, son. We're going to have to do our best to carry on. She would expect it of us. We must not shame her memory,' his mother answered him gently.

David doubted that they would succeed but did not contradict her. For the first time in his life, he felt close to her. The two of them sat listening to the howling wind outside, with nobody to comfort them in their time of bereavement except the raucous laughter of hyenas and the hooting of an owl on top of their house.

It was a menacingly dark and violent night, befitting the departure of such one as Lakeri. It brought to David's mind all the eerie ghost stories he had been told as a child. He shivered and wondered whether his grandmother had already been turned into a ghost. If she were, she would haunt him if he ever strayed from what she had brought him up to be. He looked at his mother, frightened. His mother held out her arms to him into which he eagerly rushed; his feelings of distaste at her unsightly face forgotten.

'Before Kaaka died, she told me that you got burnt while trying to rescue me from a burning house,' David disclosed.

Erina nodded and clasped him to her bosom more tightly, reliving the horrifying experience.

'I'm sorry, Mama, so sorry for everything.'

'Don't distress yourself, son. I was happy to do it and I'd do it all over again if necessary,' his mother assured him.

'I'll never be able to repay you.'

'Just be happy, David; that's all I want from you. Make me proud of you. I know you can.'

'I'll try, Mama, I'll try. I'll also try not to be ashamed of you,' he blurted and then gasped with fear. He had not meant her to know that.

'It's all right, David, I don't blame you. I'm also ashamed of myself, you know,' she confessed and tried, unsuccessfully, to quash the memory of that horrific night of the fire which still haunted her dreams after thirteen long years.

*

One day, back in her native village of Birombe, Erina went to the trading centre to buy paraffin and a box of matches, which, with a new baby in the house, she needed at night more than usual. Before going, she asked her husband to keep an eye on her sleeping infant of three months in case he woke up in her absence. When she came back an hour later, she was met by billowing columns of thick smoke a short distance from the homestead. Their grass-thatched house was up in flames and her husband and baby were nowhere to be seen. Fearing the worst, Erina leapt into the inferno against warnings from onlookers. But she could not let her beloved husband and son die in the fire without attempting to save them.

After imperilling her life, she managed to rescue her baby but there was no sign of her husband. She was so badly burnt that she spent six months in hospital, suspended between life and death. The pain was so intense and the damage to her face so extensive that she could not help feeling that death would be a welcome release. But because of her mother's encouragement and her own desire to see the son she had sacrificed so much for grow into a man, she hung on to life. 'Your baby needs you since your husband has abandoned you both,' her mother told her emphatically.

'My baby needs me' became Erina's reason to live, to go on day after day even when she felt at the lowest of the low. 'My baby needs me,' she would repeat it as a talisman and felt strengthened to go on with her accursed existence.

So to Kagadi with her mother and baby boy she went in search of a new start. A new start, with her face gnarled and warped like the back of an ancient tree, how could there ever be a new start for her?

But now with her thirteen-year old son, looking at her without flinching for the first time, Erina felt that, indeed, a new start was possible. For David's sake, she would try to overcome her deepest fears and despairs and face the world more boldly. She knew that people would still reject her and recoil from her because of her deformity, but she prayed that among the multitudes of people out there, she could find at least one person to befriend and make her feel that in spite of everything, she was still a member of the human race. That was all she asked for, now that her mother, the only person who knew the real person behind the shell, was gone.

She looked at her scared son and hastened to reassure him. 'I know that because I'm a cripple I don't inspire much confidence in you, David, but I assure you that you can count on me from now on to do the best I can for you. I'm still young and strong, no matter what the world may think of me; together we shall overcome whatever challenges that may come our way. God gave you a good brain David; use it to make a better life for yourself than your grandmother and I have been able to give you.'

'I pray that when I grow up I can repay a little of what you've given me, mother,' he said earnestly and made a silent vow to keep his promise.

His mother looked at the tear-stained, as-yet-unformed face and caught a glimpse of the man David would be in ten or so years' time. Do not let the likeness be more than physical, she prayed silently and felt her mother's presence strongly. Erina knew then that although Lakeri was physically gone, her wish to shape David into a responsible person and inculcate in him those values she deemed essential to turn out a wholesome man still applied and it was her duty to carry on from where she left off. 'I know you will, son, with God's help, you will,' she told him smiling confidently. But all this was still in the distant future.

*

David did well at school and kept to the straight and narrow path his grandmother had brought him to know. But although at university he manfully endeavoured to stay uncontaminated, the pressure from his peers wrestled him down and so he joined in with the fun of women and drink. Still he confined his relationships with the opposite sex to the 'hit-and-run' kind only, determined that nobody should ever find out about the *Kagadi Buhamiro*. And then he met Kimuli and everything changed. Everything, that is, except his resolve to keep his secret a secret.

Kimuli was a persistent young woman who liked to have her own way. She had decided that the reserved handsome young man from the land of milk and honey, as Kaarokarungi was lyrically called, was the man for her. But although the feeling seemed mutual, David seemed to have barricaded himself behind an impenetrable wall. It was this barrier she needed to overcome in order to know the inner man. The more time they spent together, the better her chances of bringing his defences down.

Now completely unaware that their thoughts veered in different directions, Kimuli asked, 'What are you doing for Christmas, David?'

Fearing that she was about to invite him to spend it with her family, David immediately became wary. He recalled, with a bitter taste in his mouth, the last and only time Kimuli took him to her home for lunch and what a disaster it had turned out to be.

Kimuli came from a well-to-do Ganda family, the type referred to as the middle class in the Uganda of today. But it was not until David stood before the intimidating, double-storied brick mansion in one of Kampala's exclusive suburbs reserved for foreign diplomats, top army men and affluent businessmen that he appreciated how exceedingly rich Kimuli's father was.

David, in his second-hand clothes from a down town market, started to feel like a fish out of water. He felt completely overwhelmed, and matters were not helped by the instant dislike he seemed to have inspired in Kimuli's father, a pompous, typical *mafuta mingi* bully, who wore his corpulent body like a badge of success.

After David was introduced and shown to a seat, his host offered him a bottle of Nile Special and proceeded to grill him in order to establish his background.

'Are you related to Moreka Buhamiro, the Managing Director of Dama Enterprise Uganda Ltd?'

David had never heard of Moreka Buhamiro, let alone Dama Enterprise Uganda Ltd. 'No, I'm not,' David replied candidly.

'Where did you say you come from – Kagadi, isn't it? Then you must know a friend of mine called Batunga. He owns the largest head of cattle in the area and supplies my factory with hides and skins.'

David drew in his breath in awe. He knew of Mr Batunga, known as Byandala (very rich man) in Kagadi. 'I've heard of Mr Batunga,' he answered cautiously. It was now becoming apparent that the only way David could find favour with Mr Mukubwa was through some connection to one of the top ten rich men in the country. After many other efforts to link him to at least some peripherally nationally famous figure in Kaarokarungi hit a dead end, Mr Mukuubwa consigned David to the heap of the unworthy, ignoring him thereafter and devoting himself solely to his daughter.

Mrs Mukuubwa, a kindly but insignificant woman, did what she could to make David feel welcome, but nothing she said could restore his bashed self-esteem, which had been fragile enough to begin with.

As soon as David crept out of the wrought iron gate, he

breathed deeply with relief and felt his chest lighten. A herd of rampaging buffalos would not make him seek refuge inside that garrison; nothing would. He wondered what impact the aborted visit would have on his future relationship with Kimuli. Certainly not a positive one, he knew, especially if he were to have the temerity to ask for her hand in marriage; an idea he had toyed with, but was now convinced that it would never work.

That had been last October on Independence Day Anniversary. The memory still made him break out in a sweat and no matter how much he loved Kimuli, there were limits to what he was prepared to do for her, one of which was to stand in front of Mr Mukubwa's firing range. So he now said quickly, 'I'm thinking of going home.'

'That's wonderful, David. You can invite me to come along with you then, can't you?'

Oh, no, it's worse than I thought. David goggled at her alarmed. 'But your family will expect you home for the holiday surely!'

'Don't worry, I can handle my family. I'd rather be with you, anyway, than with my boring old family.'

'My mother's shy and might not appreciate our turning up without notice,' he offered as a last resort in an effort to discourage her.

'I'm a nurse, remember, and I know how to handle all sorts of people,' Kimuli assured him.

'Look,' David said slowly, determinedly, 'the idea is not a good one right now, Kimuli. I'd rather we let things take their course.'

'By which you mean that I'm rushing you, isn't it.? I'm not proposing a major take-over of your life, for heaven's sake,' Kimuli added exasperated. 'I simply want to spend a day or two with you in the country, where I can get to know you better.'

'I'd like to know you better Kim, but believe me, a visit to my home is not only untimely, it could also turn out to be very critical to our relationship,' David warned.

'That's what I'm hoping for.' She kept up the pressure until David gave in.

*

When David went home, he was surprised at the changes his mother had managed to affect on the small place in the one year he had not been home. The house now had an iron roof instead of a grass one and the walls were plastered with cow-dung mixed with lime soil. It looked quite presentable and fitted in well with their other neighbours' humble shelters.

'It looks great, Mother!' he enthused; although by city standards, it was still pathetic. But he had never seen his mother so happy. The glowing look on her face almost made one overlook her deformity, but it was there all right, and David wondered what Kimuli would make of it and the pitiful place he called home. He'd find out soon enough when she joined them for Christmas.

His mother received the news of Kimuli's visit with apparent equanimity although, inside, she felt apprehensive at receiving a total stranger into her home.

David had given Kimuli clear directions on how to get to Kagadi by bus. He suspected she would not have told her parents where she was going to spend Christmas, hence the need to use public transport. There was a very good bus service and many taxis stopped within walking distance of his home. He had arranged to meet her at the bus stop.

Two hours before David was due to meet Kimuli's bus on Christmas morning, Erina remembered she had forgotten to buy sugar and sent him some two kilometres away for it. 'We must have evening tea. Don't worry, you'll be in time to meet the bus.' David was worried, but not about being on time to meet the bus. He was worried about what Kimuli would think of his mother, his home...

Erina had just finished putting *matooke* on the fire when there was a loud knock on the front door. Who can be, she wondered, hurriedly wiping her hands on her long work dress. She hurried inside the house to open the front door to whoever was knocking. Perhaps it was one of David's friends.

It was one of David's friends all right but not any of those she had in mind. It is debatable whose astonishment was greater at the appearance of the other. The tall beautiful girl in a pair of blue jeans and a red T-shirt with strings of braided hair over her shoulders or the woman with the face of a gargoyle and the body of a human in a dirty, colourless, long dress? Kimuli's face turned ashen at the apparition and she stifled a cry of alarm. The small holdall she was carrying dropped to the ground as both her hands flew to her chest, her terrified eyes staring. 'I…I…' she tried to speak but no words came out.

Erina had advantage over her visitor in that she had been expecting her and could therefore guess her identity. She started to smile reassuringly but on seeing the reaction of the young woman's face she quickly closed her mouth. Her damaged red eye, deeply encased in the wrinkled folds of flesh, flapped madly up and down in confusion as she realised what sight she presented to the poor girl without her veil. She was now in the habit of discarding it in the confines of her home while working. Mustering all her courage, she made an attempt at welcoming the visitor, saying, 'You must be Kimuli. We were not expecting you for another hour or so. That's why David was not at the station to meet you.'

Without attempting to hide her revulsion, Kimuli made no response. Nothing in the four years of her working as a medical nurse had prepared her for the sight before her. She took an instinctive step backwards as if fearing close contact might contaminate her.

'Come in, Kimuli. David won't be long,' Erina said with an effort. She was used to people's shocked reactions on seeing her for the first time, but the manner in which David's girl was behaving was unnerving. She wished she would stop staring at her as if she was a freak – oh why doesn't David come and rescue me, she cried inwardly.

'No, thank you. I don't know the David you're talking about. I've just lost my way.' In saying so, Kimuli stooped and picked up her bag and edged away slowly, as one would from a dangerous wild beast. A few metres away from the house, she turned to a nearby bush to empty the bile that had been building up in her throat ever since she set eyes on the hideous creature. She wiped her mouth with the back of her hand before resuming her journey, almost at a run.

Erina watched the retreating figure with sadness. She felt more sorry for her son than for herself. So when David came back half an hour later and announced that he was going to meet their visitor, she did not tell him that the visitor had been and gone.

'I don't understand it,' David said two hours later, after the last bus from Kampala had passed him without stopping. 'Kimuli has not appeared up to now.'

'Perhaps something came up to make her change her mind,' his mother said tactfully.

David worried for a while in case Kimuli had lost her way. But when it became apparent that she was not likely to turn up at all, he experienced a sense of relief that the meeting between the two women had not taken place after all.

THE WEDDING BALL
Ulysses Chuka Kibuuka

Youthful Major Michael Mairikiti and his fiancée Doris Namanda
ate a late lunch at Arua Park,where the Gimara woman from the
West Nile cooked grilled game meat in ground sesame seed paste.
Mairikiti suspected the game meat was off when he felt the first
pang of gradually increasing sharp pain in his left testicle, which
struck just as they stepped out of the restaurant. A long time ago
when he was a teenager, a buffalo died near their home and
several families shared the free meat. What saved the Mairikiti
family was that as Adventists, their religion barred them from
eating what was called 'unclean' meat, which included meat of
wild and dead animals. Several homes buried large numbers of
family members and others ended up in a hospital thirty miles
away where they were confined to bed for weeks. What if the
Gimara restaurateur had bought her meat from poachers that had
skinned a sick animal that they had found dead?

The couple was time-barred as up the street, the costumier
Margot Yiga was awaiting them at her Magomago Fashions
Shoppe, where they were to select Namanda's dresses and gowns
for their wedding in a fortnight's time.

But now Mairikiti's mind was divided as he thought of his pain.
'My testicle of all things?' – he asked himself with a little secret
rueful smile on his lips. 'At this time of all times!' At that time he
hoped it was a simple thing; stabs of pain in his testicle were not
strange or rare. He knew a thing or two about ailing testicles in
fact, having been hospitalised at one time eleven years previously.

The pain moved gradually, progressing, as it seemed, in an
upward wave with every step he took. At one point it grew so

sharp he felt it like a blunt needle stab at a spot in his lower abdomen with crude force and he nearly bent double with its effect. But he said nothing of it to his girlfriend as they walked up the incline of Johnston Street toward Pioneer Mall.

At Antonio's, before the City Square, Mairikiti told Namanda about the pain through tightly clenched teeth and led her off the pavement into the restaurant. He did not mention his testicles, not wanting to cause her unnecessary anxiety. *Antonio's* specialised in heavily fried, greasy Lebanese food. Since they had just finished lunch, Namanda knew they hadn't entered *Antonio's* for a snack. But it made her notice the extent of her fiancé's discomfort. They sat on the cold seats made of multicoloured squares of ceramic tiles. The tabletops where they rested their forearms were made of the same material as the seats.

Mairikiti sat with his legs wide apart, a look of utter embarrassment over his face. Carefully and furtively, so as not to attract other patrons' attention to his plight, he eased the belt of his trousers several notches, undid the single button of his corduroy trousers and pulled the zipper all the way down. His eyes wandered around the place to see if he was being watched as he edged a hand down the front of the waistband. For underpants, he had worn sports shorts with loose sewn-in underpants of mesh, a thing he did occasionally without thought. When a doctor told him weeks later that one of the remedies for torsion was a tight pair of underpants, he realised the loose things he wore might have been responsible for his dreadful tribulations of that day. He pushed the tips of his right hand down, lifting himself slightly off the seat, and edging his fingers beneath his stubbly testicles, which felt very hot and tender to the fingers.

Namanda was watching him with a troubled, doubtful look on her pretty dark mahogany face. Mairikiti's face was a mixture of anguish, worry, hopelessness and wonder. The smile, albeit mournful, should not have been there, but then it was not quite a smile; it appeared as though he was laughing inwardly at himself. Unknown to her, the man that would be her wed husband in twelve days' time, had his fingers busy massaging his testicles and his mind was not impressed with their passiveness. The mass of large and small veins that represented his right testicle was the first thing he felt with the fingers. There was no significant feeling there and this did not surprise him unduly for it had been like that for nearly a decade. But the left testicle was heavy, hot and bulgy – verily bruised. Mairikiti lifted his buttocks a little bit more from the seat to loosen his testicles from a fold in the soft mesh of his inner shorts and sat back slowly after ensuring some little amount of comfort. But the pain did not subside even though it seemed to have reached its peak.

'Maikolo, you do not seem all right,' Namanda spoke gently to him. 'Kiki, swiiti? Where is that pain…?'

'I am okay, *kabite*, just some little ache that has disabled my walking. I believe it will go. All I need is to sit down a bit and rest my body.' He pulled out his mobile phone and dialled a number. 'I should call Miro. He is a man of quick solutions, and he has some money that I can use in an emergency. '*Yyee*, Miro,' he spoke into the phone. 'I am at *Antonio's* food pub. I have a very, very serious problem. Can you find me here?'

'A *very, very* serious problem? *Sente?*'

'It's a medical problem; yes, and money too. *Ojja?*'

'Of course I am coming. I am not far from the Pioneer Mall. Give me three minutes.'

'*Oyanguwako!* The faster the better, Miro.'

They sat and waited, she staring at him – wishing he could put on a bright smile and announce the problem was over; he looking sheepishly away from her, over the heads of the clientele in *Antonio's*, wishing the pain would subside or go away altogether so that he could announce to her he was well and ready to move again. Margot Yiga's shop closed at four-thirty. They still had an hour or two even.

'What exactly is *it?*' Namanda asked and before Mairikiti could answer, Miro's large, tall figure darkened the main entrance of the pub. He looked around and located the two, ambling his way to them through the closely constructed seats. They exchanged quick salutations and Mairikiti introduced Namanda.

'Your fiancée! Is she really a soldier also?'

'Corporal Doris Namanda is in the Information-Technology Directorate with me. But she is attached to field artillery. We've dated for now six months.'

'Ayyaa! Who have you not told of her anyway? Everybody is looking eagerly toward this wedding next month.' Miro shot Namanda a glance and told her. 'I would like to look at you in combat garb. You must be more smashing even.'

'We are doing it in the military style so you will see me in uniform.'

'Ha! With glittering swords shooting upwards at the sky and you walking underneath? I can't wait to see you chaps. But Major, what is it? You talked of a medical problem, yet you look okay.'

'*Leka naawe*! Do I look okay? Thank God for that. I feared everybody in the restaurant was able to see my devil of a discomfiture! It is my testicle.'

There was an abrupt brittle silence between the trio.

'Your what?' Miro exploded. 'What's wrong with your testicles?'

Namanda changed her position on the seat to stare at her fiancé with apparent shock. 'You never told me, Maikolo!'

'Testicle. Just one. It's swollen to the size of a chicken's egg. And painful *nnyo'nnyo*! But I told you about the pain, *kabite*; not the location though. I could not tell you that right away, hoping it might relent. You can imagine how embarrassed I feel even as I talk. *Bannange nfa*, I am in dire shit.'

'But you are seated here doing nothing - seek a doctor!'

'You could have told me what the thing was, Maikolo,' Namanda said plaintively. 'I suspected there was a problem and yet....'

'How could I tell you, Doris, *mukwaano*? It is such a touchy situation in such a funny region too. Now I can't even walk, so how do I get to see a medico? We sat here so that – because I hoped the pain might ease. It's still there and I am worried to death. I am utterly disabled.'

'And you don't have a car, a major in the mighty national army! And of course you cannot have money since it is not yet month's end.'

'Don't rub it in, fellow; actually I had deposited all the cash I had on me with Miss Margot Yiga for Doris' wedding things. I only remained with the fare to return us to the barracks.'

'My *mulamu*,' Miro addressed Namanda. 'Is your army actually like that or is my brother here pulling my leg when he says, as he likes to say often, that a sergeant in Idi Amin's army was a lot better off than a senior officer in this once-upon-a-time guerrilla outfit that is the Ugandan army!'

Namanda laughed and said; 'I was born the day General Idi Amin was ousted from power by the Tanzanians, so I cannot know how much those sergeants earned in wages. But I hear that complaint very often. It makes Idi Amin like an angel of sorts!'

'Ah, you are right, sister in law. You cannot divulge matters military to a nosy relative, can you? Well, *baaba*, can't you think of a doctor?'

'Maybe the pain will ease a little bit more and then I will be able to think straighter. Let's sit for a while.'

They sat, with Namanda attempting to bring up some conversation, to take her fiancé's thoughts off his testicle. She wondered what the pain was like; was it like the pain in a hurting breast? She winced inwardly at the imagination.

'Maybe I should seek out a clinic,' said Mairikiti. 'Even if I don't have enough money on me. Maybe I could take a taxi to Mulago Government Hospital where things are free. My – the pain doesn't let up. I called you Miro for help; so what are you going to do about my problem?'

'I know a doctor; a certain old doctor on Entebbe Road. Dr Lwanga is his name and he is a general practitioner. Perhaps….'

'Why not a simple clinic… with a medical assistant? Doctors are expensive. I told you I don't have enough money on me.'

They sat silently for a while. Then Mairikiti said 'It can be serious you know. In fact I am a little frightened – you see I read somewhere… I've read about this sort of pain – pain in the testicle. It was in a medical book a long time ago. It can end up in your testicle being removed surgically to save your life.' He then lowered his voice a decibel and added. 'Moreover, I have only one testicle.'

Namanda stared at her fiancé openmouthed. '*Kiki, Maikolo!*'

Miro's mouth stood open too, a man clearly stunned. 'What did you just say?'

'I have only one testicle. The other one went away – I mean, melted away after a bout of mumps eleven years ago.'

'Melted – melted away!' Namanda was petrified on the cold

marble seat. 'I – you have never told me about that. It is not true.'

'*Kituufu nnyo*. I don't go around saying it, that is all.'

Miro got up and, with his hands clasped round his temples in agitation, paced up and down the then less crowded restaurant floor.

'But I would have known. It's not like I don't know your – umm… testicles. I've always touched them.' Namanda pronounced testicles as 'testacles'.

'Not clinically though – you never did. And you wouldn't know, Doris, *mwaana wattu*.'

'But doesn't that mean…? Michael, you are not so fussy in bed. The removal… absence of testicles would make you like… like castrated goats.'

'One testis is okay for sex. In castration both testicles are removed.'

'And now you say you have only….' She cut her sentence short as Miro stopped by their seat and sat down heavily.

Namanda stood up quickly looking at her fiancé with utmost urgency in her eyes which she had screwed nearly shut. She tugged at his arm saying 'what are we doing here? What about that doctor on Entebbe Road your brother mentioned. I know Dr Lwanga too. We once took my mother there. I believe he might recognise me and give us treatment on credit should Miro have no money. I will call my brother and ask him to call Lwanga and explain. Please, we cannot wait.'

'Look, nothing would make me refuse any such offer at this juncture. But I don't even know that I can walk all the way to Entebbe Road. Which part of Entebbe Road is it anyhow?'

Miro said; 'Opposite Uganda Railways goods shed, below the Nakasero Tabligh Mosque.'

'The old unfinished building?'

'Yes. There. We can take *bodabodas*.'

'You think so?'

'Yes,' said Namanda and Miro in unison. 'It's not expensive.'

'But *bodabodas* are so – unreliable.'

'That's my worry too,' said Namanda. 'We'll warn the riders to move carefully. You think your er… testacles… can take it?'

Mairikiti looked at the two appreciatively, grateful to know they truly cared and sympathised. 'Ours… you and I, *kabite*. I think the pain isn't that bad anymore, but it is there. Maybe the scrotum has gone numb by now, or maybe it is wishful thinking on my part. Let us try it. Maybe the motorcycle's carrier won't aggravate matters.'

'The hurt cannot be as bad as doing nothing about it,' Miro was impatient. '*Tugende mangu-mangu* without wasting more time.'

They walked out of *Antonio's* with Namanda and Miro attempting to help him walk, but he shrugged them off, not wanting to bring attention to himself. The pain was now a dull ache that no longer stabbed at his lower tummy.

The streets were rowdy with noise from jostling pedestrians, hawkers of all nature of merchandise, taxi touts, heavy luggage carriers, car horns, *bodaboda* motorcycle exhaust pipes and pneumatic drills and hammers echoing away within a building being reconstructed across the street. The air was clogged with motor vehicle exhaust fumes, sandy dust wafting in billowy wind from the construction sites in the third and fourth floors of the reconstructed building and sometimes foul and sometimes aromatic smells from the kitchens of the numerous restaurants of Johnston Street.

'*Boda*,' Miro yelled. A *bodaboda* motorcycle screeched to a stop and the two helped Mairikiti to sit astride its carrier. Miro firmly held on to one side of the handlebars of the heaving machine to prevent the impatient rider from moving off even before they gave him directions. As Namanda sat herself on another machine sideways the way Ugandan women sit on motorcycles, Miro's other hand flagged down a speeding *bodaboda* and when it stopped, he said to the first cyclist; 'I will lead the way,' and jumped onto the waiting machine. They rode down William Street through thick traffic that grew even thicker when they edged their way into Ben Kiwanuka Street.

Major Michael Mairikiti jammed his lower teeth against the upper, as the pain in his scrotum seemed to shoot up with the movement of the *bodaboda*. Even though it was his wish to keep his legs wide apart for comfort, he had to keep his knees pressed to the sides of the machine to prevent them from colliding with oncoming motorcars and trucks. The bedlam that was Kampala's late afternoon traffic was thickest at the junction of Ben Kiwanuka and Janan Luwuum streets so that even the wily *bodaboda* riders were lost for solutions to beating the traffic jam.

After nearly ten minutes Mairikiti and his truly worried friends climbed the narrow staircase to Dr Lwanga's clinic.

There were two women on the sofa waiting, one very smartly dressed and elderly, and the other much younger and in simple working *kitenge* dress. As the trio came in, a door opened off a brightly lit room and a man dressed in a swanky suit walked out. A grey haired head with rimless spectacles popped out of the room surrounded by bright light and nodded at the two women seated on the sofa. As one of the women stood up, Miro said; 'Eh, Doctor!' but cut his speech when he realised he was not noticed by the old physician.

'I know this old man only too well,' said Namanda. 'He is extremely strict.'

They sat next to the well-dressed woman, who greeted them politely; '*Musiibye mutya'nno, bakulu?*'

'*Tuli bulungi, munnaffe,*' they replied in unison, as if they were really well.

Mairikiti's jaw was still clenched, fighting the pain that he still felt, albeit much less pronouncedly. Namanda stared at his face constantly while Miro glanced at him from time to time, uneasily. Then he fixed his big brother with a stare and said in a way that the well-dressed woman could not overhear: 'Why only one?'

Mairikiti threw a sideways-glance at the woman they were seated with. He said quietly; '*Tolabika kukakasa byennkugamba, nga Doris wano. Mambulugga,*'

'Look, it's not that I doubt you; I am only stupefied. *Mambulugga*! So you were serious about the mumps thing?'

'*Yee, mambulugga.* I got them – or rather they got me, eleven years ago when I laughed at a little daughter of friends of mine that had them, in Zana. I laughed at her telling her I wanted to catch them when I found her smeared with Coleman's azure blue around her gills – I mean the area they traditionally smear such things around the lower cheeks, just in front of the ear, for the sole purpose that such victims of mumps can be laughed at.'

'Uh-hm,' Miro chuckled softly. 'So you are saying that it is true that when you laugh at a person with *mambulugga* you get them?'

'I have known its verity for a number of years now because it is eleven years ago when I laughed at this little *ka-nnyazaala* Sandra Kavuyo, aged six then, when she had mumps and I contracted them. The blessed lady is now a teenager living in London with her mother and a little brother. You haven't suffered from them, Miro, have you?'

'Maybe I have, perhaps when I was a kid. I don't really remember. Mind you I am now thirty-two.'

'Me, I suffered from them when I was in primary four,' said Namanda. 'They can be really painful. You develop a very high fever.'

'Yeah,' said Mairikiti. 'It is very bad to get them above teen age. I was aged twenty-six eleven years ago when mumps attacked me. I remember everybody catching them during our adolescence in the early seventies, but not me, no. I didn't get them. They smeared Coleman's azure blue and charcoal around the lower cheeks of these chaps and whoever laughed at the sufferer got them. I don't remember whether or not I did not laugh. Anyhow I never got *mambulugga*.'

'In my *kyaalo*,' said Namanda. 'They tie a ring of raffia string round your neck below the lumps in the jaw and that is sufficient medication.'

'Yes,' said Mairikiti. 'And that is the interesting thing about African traditional medicine. That string, though tied loosely round your neck, is meant to prevent those lumps descending down your body into the lumps that are your testicles. Comparatively, but very rarely, women's ovaries may suffer the same fate as a man's balls. In older sufferers actually, or when it is believed the *mambulugga* lumps have moved past the jaw line, they tie the raffia string, a bit more tightly, round your chest. This prevents any further downward course of the disease.'

'Our African traditional mumbo jumbo, of course,' said Miro.

'No, I don't think so. You see, I refused to follow the advice given on that string; refused to have it tied round my neck. Within two days the mumps had descended to my testicles. And when I was taken to hospital the medical personnel seemed to know something about this thing descending even though it was

a bit too late for me. They made me lie on a cot whose lower end
– where the legs ended, was raised so that my head lay much
lower. Maybe that is what helped me to retain the remaining
testicle.'

'Whew!' Miro exclaimed by way of a whistle-like sound. 'Uh-
hm?'

'I was admitted to that hospital for a couple of weeks.'

'But mumps go away by themselves in a short time in all cases I
have seen,' said Namanda. 'I have never seen a hospital case.'

'Yes. When you have been intelligent enough to adhere to wise
traditional counsel from those who know these things. Many
sufferers do; I did not, headstrong me! On the other hand, when
they go down into your testicles, the fevers can be extreme, hence
the hospitalisation.'

Three more patients had come into the waiting room and joined
them on the long sofas. Namanda had walked off to the lavatory.
The well-dressed woman had gone in to see the doctor and
Mairikiti and Miro waited, the pain in the soldier's scrotum still
worrisome.'One testicle!' Miro said in a puzzled whisper. 'Do you
function?'

'Yes, thank God. Or else what would the likes of Namanda be
looking for?'

'But… I think you cannot….'

Mairikiti lowered his voice a decibel when he noticed a man
keenly interested in their conversation archly craning his neck to
listen. He said; 'You know, Miro, I recall that the first whole year
after coming from hospital, almost every woman I slept with
came back to claim I had put them in the family way. I remember
wondering that simply too many of them came up with that
claim. I helped them abort, with money you know, and advice on
which doctors to go to. But now for nearly a decade, either due
to *kisirane* from God for helping so many women to abort, not
one single lass has come offering me a pregnancy!'

'Offering you a…!'

'Claiming I put them in the family way.'

'You mean you… you wanted them to… you wanted to give
them children?'

'Naturally. Everybody wants children, more especially when

there is reason to believe you cannot have them, and…. Well, here comes Doris.'

And as Namanda made to lower herself on the sofa, the grey-haired head with rimless glasses popped out of the brightly lit room. Its owner said suavely; 'Would you like to come in please.'

They trooped into the consultation room and stood before the physician. Miro talked in a low whisper to the doctor, who rolled an eye in Mairikiti's direction. 'I know the girl,' said the doctor. 'Are you not the daughter of Salinge?'

'Yes, doctor,' replied Namanda.

'How's she?'

'She's *guluggulu*, Doctor, thanks to your medications.'

'Now, young fellow,' the doctor addressed Mairikiti. 'What's wrong with your testis?'

'Ha, Doctor; I am not young. I am turning forty in three years.'

'And what *should* I say? Tell me your problem.'

'I developed a sharp pain down there several minutes ago after having a lunch of bushbuck meat and large lump of sorghum dough. It's still there, though dull, that pain.'

'What sort of pain? Could you have accidentally sat on your scrotum or was it kind of gradual and intensifying?

'Gradually intensifying, Doctor. I had to sit some place for it to ease but….'

'Lady, you may leave us, please… or is she….'

'She's my er… my fiancée.'

'She can stay? Because I want you to remove your trousers immediately.'

'She can stay, doctor. She already….'

'Remove your trousers then, right away, man. How long did you say the onset … when did you start to experience that pain? How long ago?'

'Maybe some thirty-five minutes…. *Sikyeekyo,* Doris?'

'Thirty or thirty-five, Doctor,' Namanda said.

'Do you still feel the pain?'

'Yes. Dully though.'

The old physician's fingers were already at work, shifting and twisting the old soldier's testicles this way and that, gently. Michael Mairikiti, a very modest soldier, was too abashed to look at his two companions.

'One of your testicles is atrophied, did you know that?'

'Yes. I lost it to mumps.'

'Oo, yes. Mumps can do that. Too bad. Maybe the lady should leave us,' Mairikiti began to protest but the doctor appeared adamant. 'Please daughter of Salinge, leave us men alone.'

And when Namanda had closed the door behind her, the elderly man hurried to a desk, picked a notepad and a small red marker that he got after a greatly frantic search among things on the tabletop. He scribbled notes in medical jargon on the plain white piece of paper that bore his clinic's name and his qualifications. Then he turned the marker's tip to write thicker, bolder words at the top and at the bottom of the form: URGENT. He handed the note to the soldier, saying with urgency in voice and poise; 'You have no time to lose. Mairye Hospital is just five minutes' drive from here. But traffic jams must not delay you. So you better leave your car parked here and take a *bodaboda*. It may take you three minutes if you're lucky. Go straight to the first doctor you meet there and flash this note to them. You must be operated upon immediately or else you will lose your other testicle. Actually if you say it's been thirty-five minutes since the onset, then you have at least ten-to-fifteen minutes to undergo the operation, not more. If you delay, then the remaining testicle will be surgically removed to save your life. If you hurry the surgical operation will rectify the problem and you may perhaps keep your testicle. Hurry, young fellow. You'll find *bodabodas* down below.' All this the old doctor said pushing Mairikiti physically by the shoulder, demonstrating utmost urgency, out of his clinic.

'Sir, the money....' Miro began.

'Another time. There is no time now, fellows. Mairye Hospital *mangu-mangu*, young man.'

Mairye Hospital was one of the oldest hospitals in Kampala City. Built by the Mill Hill Fathers around the beginning of the twentieth century, it was located a stone's throw distance from the Queen Elizabeth Clock Tower on Queen's Way, which was part of Entebbe Road. In three minutes flat, the motorcyclists had dropped the trio at the hospital's entrance. They hurried into the hospital and headed for the outpatients' area where they approached a young light skinned nurse dressed in a deep pink cotton cloth uniform who introduced herself as Nurse Eliza Wanda. She was small bodied, short – about five-foot-four and stoutly built, with an accent that placed her among the Bamasaba people of Bulucheke in Eastern Uganda. They handed her Dr Lwanga's note, which she appeared not to regard as all that important as she led them to a big and tall benign looking Catholic nun dressed in silver grey, who looked at the note once and herded the trio, along with Eliza Wanda, to a section of the hospital where a bespectacled man addressed as Dr Tamale, in white coat and toting a stethoscope, received them.

He looked at the note and frowned 'Which is it, you?'

Mairikiti nodded and was immediately helped onto a table where the nurse began to remove his brown corduroy trousers. All were asked to leave the room except the nun and the nurse. Dr Tamale and a Dr Ssegamwenge cursorily examined his testicles by pushing them this way and that, and one of them instructed the nun to telephone a Dr Manuel Baine. 'This is Baine's field,' he said. Then, to the nurse in pink, he said. 'Remove the rest of his clothes, dress him in gown, and take him to Room G in the theatre and salve this area of the crotch. Tell sister to book him in ward one-eight. And Eliza, don't forget to shave away that stubble of pubic hair. I do hope Dr Baine comes quickly enough. If he doesn't, you and I can make a go at it, no?' he asked Dr Ssegamwenge with a cheerful laugh. 'Who did you come with, Major?'

'Ah, my fiancée and my brother.'

'Fiancée!' Tamale said, wincing. 'Oh, *Katonda mu'ggulu*!'

'Mmmm, God in heaven indeed!' said Mairikiti with a weak chuckle. 'That is the irony of things. We are to wed in a fortnight's time. I hope you attend the funeral – ah, sorry, wedding. Please, call them in.'

The two young doctors shared the joke, after which Dr Tamale asked 'Even the girl...!'

'*Especially the girl*. She must know if I am to become a eunuch.'

'Not necessarily, Major; we still think it can be saved. I had at first suspected a case of epididymitis, which is usually caused by some of the rampant diseases we have around, like gonorrhea or tuberculosis. It is true your condition is quite grave. You see the... each testis is suspended from a pair of chords that transport the supply of blood from the scrotum and connect it to the sperm ducts. Now this sort of problem mostly afflicts much older or much younger people, not men of thirty-seven. These two chords may twist – actually entangle and in the process suffocate each other hence cutting off the blood supply. If reported to a surgeon quickly – say within forty minutes – not much more, the surgeon will cut the scrotum and disentangle those chords manually. If there is considerable delay, the lack of blood flow in these chords – veins mind you, may cause something like gangrene. The veins die and cannot be resurrected. In that case you lose the testicle. But all this now depends solely on the punctuality of Dr Baine. That's why we – Dr Ssegamwenge and I - might come in to operate. But I must tell you it would be better if it was Dr Baine because none of us has ever carried out such an operation before.'

Mairikiti was in no position to digest what young Dr Tamale was explaining mostly because he did not like it one bit. As they led him to theatre, Namanda and Miro followed them. She asked him; 'Are they going to operate?'

'Certainly. They are operating either to disentangle the chords that keep my balls hanging in place so that those chords can re-supply blood to that area, or if we are late as it quite easily looks to be the case, they are operating to remove the dead testicle that was denied blood supply for too long.'

'O *Katonda mu'ggulu,* no!' Namanda stopped dead in her steps. 'No, Maikolo, for God's sake!'

'It all depends on a certain Dr Manuel Baine, Doris. He is their expert on testicles, not God.'

Miro cut in to ease the tension 'I called the relatives to tell them of your plight,' said Miro.

'You didn't tell them about the testis?'

'I did not exactly say what the implications are. But *testis* they know it is. Where are we headed?'

'Room G. If that Dr Manuel Baine comes early enough I may be saved. If he delays, two not extremely well qualified interns might have me for their practicals. The good thing is that they are all so honest about it, these wonderful chaps.'

Alone in the dimly lit Room G, Mairikiti lay on his back on the operating table with a stream of thoughts coursing through his mind. All these thoughts concerned his manhood. Several years ago when he was an adolescent at school, boys and men used to say 'If I became impotent, I would not hesitate to commit suicide.' Now there he was, recalling that's what he himself used to swear.

As he lay on his back on that cold table with the grey oilskins draped over its top, he willed his manhood to come to his carnal rescue. Still sensing on his skin the salve that had been smeared all over his crotch by the nurse, his brain feverishly wondered about an erection, willing his body to conjure up one. He flexed his lower body – clenching the muscles of the buttocks and thighs, vigorously, so as to invigorate his crotch into an action of sorts that would awaken his penis into voluntary movement. Any movement there, even a slight twitch, might have elated his ego; his masculinity. But there was not even a flicker of flame in his groin, his manhood.

At thirty-seven, Mairikiti was young, and the increasingly definite idea that he might never enjoy the feeling of an erection ever again in his life frightened him mortally. The thought that only other men and not him might, within a short time from then, be the only enjoyers of his Doris Namanda, was justification enough for him to fulfill the abominable thing they used to swear during his adolescence. For the umpteenth time he noted that not less than three of the brown bottles on a rack opposite the operating table had on them the word 'poison' labeled below the name of the stuff. The pain in his crotch was now only felt with the imagination that it had been some fifty minutes earlier on Johnston Street. But whereas it never frightened him at the time because of his ignorance as to the gravity of the situation, now he was terrified by the delay of the surgical operation. Fifty-plus minutes had now passed since he left that Gimara woman's restaurant at Arua Park and the doctors had seemed to mean it when they said he had to be operated within less than that time or he would lose his 'remaining' testicle.

There was no one to ask about the whereabouts of the Dr Manuel Baine or whether or not the operation had been aborted for one reason or another. He could not move out of Room G because actually, they had told him not to. Moreover he was dressed in nothing but a simple olive green gown that barely reached his knees. He kept wondering where Namanda and Miro were.

Another half hour later the doctor had not shown up.

Major Michael Mairikiti touched his genital area once. The viscosity of the salve was thick still but crusted in some places. He touched his limp, pallid penis and his fingers kneaded its flabby flesh. All he could feel in there was a bunch of soft veins like large earthworms. All dead. No feeling of life at all. So there he was, impotent and neglected. The doctors had condemned him to a life of impotence.

Maybe they hated him knowing he was an army officer. They might hate the army and deliberately condemn a soldier to punish the institution. If they punished them one by one they may have their back on the institution they hated. Most Ugandans hated the army for one reason or another, but more especially for past mistakes committed by dictatorial regimes that utilised soldiers to traumatise the civilian community. Why had they condemned him? He checked himself quickly; were his deprecating thoughts… his scapegoating, a result of his utter hopelessness?

As he lay there, tears streaming slowly down one cheek, the door to Room G opened and he quickly removed his hand from his groin. The light skinned nurse Eliza Wanda stood there, framed in the entrance.

Mairikiti's heart, his entire body, suffered some form of shock. He did not immediately realise the shock or the thrilling feeling that followed in its wake. Somewhere along the brightly lit corridor there was commotion with a woman saying loudly; 'I am an army officer and I demand to see him immediately your gross criminal negligence notwithstanding.' Doris Namanda's voice was obvious to Mairikiti and he said to the nurse, still staring at her lower body, 'Why not let my fiancée in?' He did not seem to recognise his voice due to the thrills ringing and buzzing in his ears.

Eliza Wanda left the room, smiling politely and closing the door behind her. She had exchanged her uniform for a light, cream cotton dress with small sporadically placed dark red and yellow flowers with tiny aquamarine leaves. She clutched a ladies' black leather handbag on an arm and a small stainless steel tray with syringes, scalpels, gauze, cotton wool, ampoules and vials in another. In the whole three seconds she had stood framed in the doorway she had just shut, with the bright fluorescent light in the corridor behind her, Major Michael Mairikiti's life had taken a new turn. In those three seconds of her standing in the doorway, a wide inverted V of fluorescence separated Wanda's light cotton dress in the middle showing her dark stout thighs and small, wide hips as if she had no clothing on. She smiled innocently and responded to him 'We are very sorry Major Mairikiti, but only medical personnel can enter the theatre.' She placed the tray on a stainless steel rack. 'Unfortunately the epididymitisist could not be located....'

'The what...?'

'Epididymitisist. Dr Baine. So Doctors Tamale and Ssegamwenge will be coming in presently to operate. We are very sorry, Sir. And perhaps I can convince them to allow your fiancée in. But she must be given sterile clothing and footwear to enter here.'

Mairikiti had now sat up, leaning on an elbow. Wanda saw the stunned look, as though the man was emerging from a dream. The voice of his fiancée was now outside the theatre door. The nurse's attention was no longer divided between the wrangling party outside Room G and her patient. Her eyes nearly popped out as they focused on the short olive green gown that she had dressed Mairikiti in, which had lifted at the front as though some hot rod beneath it was seeking desperate freedom. The man covered himself with the edge of an oilskin sheet that he quickly grabbed from the table he now sat on. With his torso against the wall, the ghost of a jubilant smile had invaded his face, seemingly brightening the dimly lit theatre. He was breathless when he sat away from the wall and blurted: 'Where are my trousers, Nurse, please.'

The door swung open on hissing hinges before she could

respond and three heads one of them Namanda's, struggled, fighting to enter the theatre. The two male heads whose owners wore white coats tried to ensure Wanda remained out of the room. With its thick afro-style hair bobbing up and down and from side to side, Namanda's head seemed to be winning the battle for Room G.

'Let her in please Dr Tamale... ah, Dr Ssegamwenge. There is no longer a need for that operation it appears. Look!'

They all looked, and lo! Major Michael Mairikiti was beaming at them mirthfully, his eyes unabashedly looking from them to his lap several times. Doris Namanda's belligerent, tearful face was a spectacle to behold as it gradually transformed itself from an angry mask, slowly into a wild, bright smile, as she rushed to the surgical table and without shame groped for the grey oilskins in Mairikiti's lap.

THE GOOD SAMIA MAN
Kelvin Odoobo

Your home in Kampala is all but three clumsily erected rooms; a stuffy sitting room, too wide a bedroom for your liking and a store the size of a generous corridor, which by your generation has been baptised a bachelor's kitchen. A cheap microwave from China, a scarcely used plastic utensils' rack from Kenya and a rubbish pail with the stale remains of last week's macaroni at its bottom, is all there is to the state of the kitchen. You live in Kampala's suburbia, a typical twenty-first century slum, with hundreds of television antennas prodding the air above the rusting tin roofs, all struggling for breath and space. Chaos is the only form of arrangement here. One would never guess that in front of your brick-walled excuse of an 'apartment' block is a neighbourhood of mud shacks lying between gutters of filth.

You step, hop and jump over puddles of mucky, putrid water, polythene bags full of garbage and liquid shit - disposable toilets - trying to act all immaculate, avoid soiling your new fake Gucci boots. Thereafter, when you arrive at the *matatu* stage, you rearrange your second-hand tie, pretending that you didn't have to jump over what you jumped over to get to where you are - the story of your life.

The *matatu* tout announces his hiked Friday-morning fare. Frowns appear on the faces of market women; gloom tortures the young enthusiastic spirits of school children, misery saturates the aching hungry stomachs of industrial labourers, barely disguising the current state of the Ugandan economy. You do not fret. What is five hundred shillings if it cannot even buy a bottle of your favourite malt? You hop in the co-driver's seat after slapping the backrest lightly, careful not to soil your white Van Heusen shirt or your day, and carry on pretending to be rich.

As the driver negotiates the endless patches of tarmac, flanked by enormous potholes, sloshing with dirty water, with the confidence of a mad man who has claimed the garbage pit for his home, you begin to roll through that PowerPoint presentation in your head – the one your under-qualified boss wants to present at the poverty eradication talk shop of the Ministry Of Disaster Preparedness he has planned. The World Bank (read: plenty of free money) will be in attendance along with 'serious' humanitarian NGOs like yours whose mission statement goes 'To build the capacities of war-stricken communities through co-ordination, lobbying, advocacy and training.' You know that NGOs like yours do nothing more than hiring enterprising graduates like you to write good project proposals for Bretton Woods's institutions or donor countries who care less about your country and more about their jobless consultants they want to send to bleed your country to death, so your boss gets to line his pockets with thousands of crisp new dollar notes.

The loud mouthed disc jockey on the car stereo is rapping, 'Can you imagine HIV patients are expiring because they can't get ARVs and the government leeches are using Global Fund money to import the latest Mitsubishi Pajero models to fit their ugly government stomachs and their mistress's huge behinds into them?' You scoff when most of the passengers chuckle in approval, one even going ahead to quote a holy book: 'Man eateth where he worketh'. These are the same people who almost weep when they learn the fare is only five hundred shillings up. They seem to forget their daily quandary rather hastily.

That is, except the buxom woman seated next to you, fiddling with the noisy fading buttons of her ageing Nokia - 'darling, jst gt a cal dat grandma's sis is dead. Off 4 burial til Sunday, Luv, Candy' - before discretely arranging a rendezvous at the 'usual place'. Probably with the husband of a woman who is of the knowledge that he is off to a weekend long company retreat in the Ssese islands or Lake Bunyonyi. It makes you wonder if man is not just another beast in the wild, fucking the next seductive woman then going back home to profess his marital vows and how he fell in love with his wife, for life! You smile and thank God that your lie will be less ashen.

You meet the boss in the office kitchen and immediately feign a sombre mood when you report the demise of your only remaining paternal uncle, who in your culture is actually your elder father. Having been childless, you, his brother's first born, is in line to perform his funeral rites (and inherit his young attractive wife along the way, her muscles still hold the curves up in the significant places). This, by the way, is a foolproof excuse to get weeklong leave from work. Since you have made the presentation ready for him to recite, you only need a full salary advance for next month, since your October salary all went to clear that loan you took to buy the 21 inch flat screen TV. He empathises, but mumbles under his breath about how Africa is soon going to end up all empty, with only graves and nobody left to attend the frequent colourful funeral feasts. Not with uncles and aunties and mothers and fathers kicking the bucket all the time, sometimes twice in the same month. By the way, for the record, it was your real mother in April, your stepmother in July and the elder sister to your stepmother in August, before your late mother's stepmother decided that her time was up in September and walked into the lake in the middle of the night. And so you know, your family has healthy population growth figures, with the peak of baby-making falling around the January long rains season, so there is no real risk of family extinction or genetic death.

Soon, in the rickety worn-out Isuzu bus, you are suspended precariously between a breastfeeding expecting woman with a toddler standing between her legs and an annoying man who keeps yelling into his brick of a cell phone, about how he has just met His Excellency the President to discuss the proposed Samia kingdom, like the President was some sort of kingdom-dishing out god. Loads of flesh spills freely away from his waist. His white beard threatens to hide his face completely. He is a perfect example of people who seem to live their lives totally in reverse, who think everything pre-colonial is akin to a paradise polluted by the white man's influence. Ask him about the loyal subjects who sat by patiently, mouths ajar, in wait for the king to collect enough phlegm in his mouth, so he could offload it into their buccal cavities, the royal spit, and he would easily give you a self-assured thumbs up. The sharp texture of fifty thousand shilling notes, lying in your trouser pocket, dissuades you from these inconveniences, assures you of your frontward advance, an oasis of class amidst repudiating poverty. You feel like a flourishing citizen, with a job, a lifestyle and money to spend. Especially here, you amidst them, you loathe their unsophisticated habits which they subconsciously display. Slum children are in faded, visibly overused Sunday best clothes, on their way to their villages of origin, to brag about life in the city.

You deride their Third World ways and pray that the day when you strike your own Global Fund-like killing to buy that used Lexus you keep admiring on the internet, arrives sooner rather than later, to save you from the ride-on-the-aging-bus scenario, to usher you to the leave-a-cloud-of-dust-behind-you class of citizens in your village.

When the bus slows down to a stop at Nammawojjolo, tempting smells of chicken thighs and beef barbeques suspended on sticks awash with roasted plantains in their full golden colour appear and the villager in you momentarily materialises. You brawl with the rest for a share of these and solutions of food colouring passing for naturally extracted juice. Those who can afford it, like you, buy everything even if they don't feel hungry. What is more of a show of affluence than flinging out a half-eaten snack through the window of a moving bus, at times into the face of an unfortunate bicycle rider, heavily laden with three sacks of charcoal, sending him crashing into the bush under the backbreaking weight of his luggage, or most of the time, onto the windscreen of a smaller oncoming vehicle? This is what it means to be in the young working class. Thighs and lots of bananas throw themselves at you regularly. You devour them and leave the remains on the conveyer belt for the next enthusiastic consumer. After all you live in a banana country. That stuff grows all over the place; you wouldn't guess that it came on board a ship like flea-infested rats. Your people cannot live without bananas. Every December, you see people ferrying the green bunches about. You know that the birth of Christ has been turned into a paganist ritual by savvy business people, an excuse to tear down, chomp through, annihilate bananas; steamed, roasted, fermented into wine. They even do monkey dances in banana plantations, thigh against thigh, leaning on the soft banana stems, in the comforting loose, sweet smelling loam and on drying banana fibbers, the natural odours of natural plants spicing up the natural scents of human bodies. Everybody then is going bananas, including you.

They abandon the towns and the life of eating fried cassava chips and chapatti by the dusty road and flock to the villages with their cheap used Japanese cars and clothes, to flaunt their apparent life of affluence for the eleven months they were away. You worry that one day this annual pilgrimage to the village will break that aging bridge at the Owen Falls dam and send all of you to the Nile's riverbed for the Nile perch to feast on.

You know that you are guilty of those sins too. You, the homegrown elites, with your half-baked degrees barely able to sustain yourselves away from your grandmother's mud huts. You are intellectual sheep.

At the last stop before your village, you disembark to buy three kilograms of sugar, three loaves of bread, three bars of soap, three tins of margarine, three packets of baking flour, three of everything for the three wives of your father, all smuggled from Kenya (the goods and the wives that is). How do you think they struggle to fill your plate with the sweetest, most fleshy parts of *tilapia*, the son from the city? You can do it because you grew up seeing your father doing the same. You can tell that he swells inwardly with pride when he sees you turning out so much like him. How will the women not boast in the Monday market, if the message of the heavy-laden son disembarking from the ramshackle city bus evades the vibrant rumour mill? You shun the native way of valuing a mother's reputation by her son's wealth or her daughter's bride price, but you cannot candidly eschew the customs, lest you are labelled the disloyal son.

Why did they have to send you to those prestigious schools in Buganda, that obsession with winning a place in Makerere University on academic merit? They engraved it onto your neurons! Now that you come to think of it, they wanted you to become an overeducated tribesman really, with half a dozen wives, two dozen children, a full kraal of emaciated zebu cattle and a rarely inhabited mansion in the village. You hear your father's maternal grandmother lies on her deathbed and you wonder if it is a cancer or HIV. No, they say she is too old to suffer from those kinds of things, not at ninety-eight. Some of those things found those people already here. They are not sure whether it is ninety-eight or ninety-six or a hundred-and-one. All they know is she was born about a decade after a famous English missionary was killed on the orders of the occupying king. The one whose subjects offered their wives for royal trysts and their mouths for the honour of royal saliva, like it was a royal endorsement. The disease afflicting her is more exact, much clearer than western medicine could zero in on, they say. After all, those whites came and stole our herbs, put them into their machines, claimed to have miraculously discovered more effective remedies for tropical diseases other than those that kept our forefathers in tip-top condition, coated them with chalk and sold them back to Africa. They are in no doubt; the poor woman was bewitched by her co-wife. She hails from a family of renowned witches. The thing runs through their blood – they don't have a choice when they get possessed. They had warned him not to marry her, but typical of him and his wrong-headedness, he did just that. Now see how many broken pieces of dirty Coca-Cola bottle and dry goat skin the medicine man pulled out of her belly. You ask sarcastically, and how did he do it? Did he cut her belly up?

See him. Baba, those useless white man's books are beginning to get into your head. That woman can put things into your belly just by staring at you! It's like this - she stares at you hard; her eyeballs almost popping out, as if a piece of steamed sweet potato is stuck in her throat. Never play with people who can give you *ebikhokho*. Those books cannot explain these things. Don't you know that our knowledge of such things is far much superior to what they teach you in those schools? And did you know the white man's wizardry is even more legendary than the black man's?

Baba, you need to sit with your elders so you can learn our

ways. The city is no good except for the free money you get there, after sitting in nice offices, spending the whole day on the phone and reading things on those small TVs. In our day, men used to sweat for their money. They used to till the soil and make it bear food and fruits. And all these diseases, 'slim' and all, those prostitutes from Kampala and their disrespectful manners, do not bring those Baganda women here. She licks the tip of her index finger and points to the sky. But mama, tribalism does not work these days. It is love that matters. *Nasaye mulala*, one God, I will show you my nakedness, she swears, if you dare! You should start thinking about a good Samia girl, baba, who can dig and mill cassava into flour on a grinding stone and brew tasty *malwa* for your men friends. My son, you were born a Samia and you will die a Samia man, and when that time comes, may the gods protect you, your body will have to undergo all Samia funeral rites, otherwise your spirit will be rejected in the next world.

That patch of soil next to your great-grandfather's grave feels special with all its nothingness - the blades of spear grass cutting your smooth unaccustomed, town-bred leg skin. You spend your leisure time stoning huge, inviting, red-streaked wild dodo mangoes and luscious deep purple grapevines that leave your tongue sweet and purple. Goats are foraging, bleating together with the noise of birds and crickets. Occasionally, uninvited monkeys turn up to share the spoils of nature.

It feels more like home than your so-called apartment in Kampala, energy saving bulbs and shelves full of boring management books and Luciano Pavarotti CDs you hate to listen to; a kind of music that you want to help define your 'desired' taste, instead of your 'actual' taste. Raunchy tabloids and some meaningless *wach-dis* local versions of Jamaican ragamuffin could as well just do for you. The village in which your *esimba* - your coming of age grass-thatched mud hut is cool, standing to defy those months you have spent in that rented concrete rival in town, like a faithful wife who knows that the seductive siren that is the new mistress will not outlast her, warms your bathing water, cooks your evening meal religiously, even when she knows you have gone to visit 'her' tonight. It disobeys your philosophical ideas of sub-Saharan Africa, bequeathing such unspoiled tranquillity making you wish that the clock would run back to the time when man only had to hunt and roast his meat to make his kin satisfied and happy. Not to worry about career ambitions, long term investments and pension plans. You can take a man out of the village but you cannot take the village out of the Samia man.

You know that your father is proud that you made it to Makerere, but when those nostalgic memories of the seventies revisit him, he reminds you that your Makerere is no match for what it used to be. The Ngũgĩ Wa Thiong'o's, Julius Nyerere's and the Ali Mazrui's were the real thinkers. Nowadays you fellows just cram typed handouts to regurgitate the stuff on the answer sheets and you think you are also intellectuals. What he forgets to tell you is that most of those names went there long before him. All this between sips of *malwa*, passing his drinking tube intermittently to his cousin or making an instruction to one of his grandchildren to warm the beer pot with some hot water. My father's English would make the Queen of England proud. It is that B.A. degree in English from Makerere in him speaking.

You chaps are quite lucky. In our day, our fathers never let us sit and drink with them. You would be summoned as if for some misdemeanor only to be ordered to take a brief sip, while standing. Even before you begin to savour the yeasty taste or enjoy the dreadfully tempting half paradise of the tipsy, you would be dismissed to go back and cook with your mothers.

He chuckles, giving a woman beer was like wasting it, I tell you.

The old men are gracious by letting you give them a feeling of political temperature in the city. You speak like an authority, yet you are unaware of anything political beyond the newspaper headlines – particularly with the English Premiership about to happen. Why would anyone sane want to read what the big man says about the constitution? Is he not the same one who violated what he sanctified in writing the other day as the supreme law of the land? Let the peasants to whom the power belongs mind about politics and political power. You would not care about knowing which election was to be held unless of course it came with a public holiday and an opportunity to indulge in malt.

They take turns, the *wazee*, to educate you about the clan's dramatic history full of scarcely charted migrations which surprisingly, have been remembered and handed down the generations orally, recounting the unforgettable Obote and Amin days; all those war stories of our history sound so distant, so foreign. Amidst it all someone warns you never to disrespect your elders by handling the beer tube with your female (left) hand like you are doing, which initiates more man-to-man lessons of the old. It is better for a man to die than a beer pot to break. The mother of the child, who breaks the beer pot or touches the *malwa* with paraffin or a citrus fruit, would have to brew more beer to pay for it.

I tell you. Women of days gone by knew how to obey their men, not like the ones today who want to wear the same pair of trousers as their husbands. And if a woman was caught eating chicken, rare fish or meat delicacies she would be declared to be greedy, for such foods were a preserve for men and boys. The women and girls simply had to cook and cook those foods very well. You pay attention to all this and you begin to enjoy this new sense of masculinity. This traditional kind is manlier. It does not even seem to consider the books you have read, the exams you have sat and those you have passed, like at the NGO. This is the kind some crazy women who have no respect for the God-ordained chain of command in the family - prefer to called chauvinism - such an ugly Bonapartist name. This honour, closer to the one your great-grandfather, the pagan had, was prior to some lucid aristocratic Europeans, (long before their masters had been deposed by their suffering subjects to useless grandiose palaces) who had a huge party at which they cut a cake that resembled Africa into funny shapes which in turn created countries with borders that did not exist. They did not even consider that my other uncles and aunties were going to be citizens of some 'other' country. To those drunken colonialists, the heady feeling of conquering an African kingdom and seizing vast virgin lands was akin to the giddy sensation they acquired after indulging in Vodka!

The weekend passes with those stories of old, by elderly men, and their beer, of the woman who got beaten by her husband for not serving him properly and she got sent back to her parents.

But it did not work out. He forgot he needed someone to cook for him and someone to sweep his front yard, so after two weeks he went to plead with her to come back. When he heard children racing after chickens outside the house, he assumed they had chosen one to slaughter for the venerated in-law, whose 'eighteen cows' for the bride price still held that particular clan's record. He even sent a child to remind his mother-in-law that he did not like a lot of onions in his chicken stew. They made him sick, but he would not mind a little more salt than a pinch in his chicken sauce. He obviously did not know that an epidemic of a chicken disease had invaded the fowls in the area until when he opened his special dish to discover hundreds of well salted, much despised *obuduba* - tiny silver fish. Men did not need to know such things as chicken diseases. You could not expect them to know that an entire flock of birds needed to be treated against diseases anyway. Children only chase chickens when a guest who is held in the esteem of slaughtering a chicken for him, or so he thought.

You laugh along at such old school arrogance of men and begin to think; if this was today, all men would be in jail!.

When you wash your hands after the *wazee* and congregate to devour a plateful of *esigwogwo*, a cherished back section, of scrumptiously roasted goat and a mixture of ripe fruits and hot pepper for the brave accustomed tongues, you wonder how good life would have been if your ancestors had been left to their native lives in their native paradise.

On Sunday, you wake up to the smell of fermenting millet, it is mixed with a taste of salted *bambara* fish going stale in your mouth, plus a hangover that feels like a small engine droning away inside your skull. You know you have to go to church even though you have not seen the hallowed insides of one in months. When you remember the days of your youth, when skipping church on Sundays was strictly forbidden, when you felt angelic while intoning those Swahili or Luganda rhymes, you feel guilty that church has become just another thing separate from God and matters of faith. Those were the days when you even entertained the thought of a career on the pulpit, not with that respect and adoration those fellows commanded. You memorised the ideal picture; average or above average height, a round waist with a tummy that protrudes appropriately out of the cassock, where his left hand rests as the other one waves and shakes eager hands, offerings blessings for free. Christ himself, through his servant.

When they sing those never-changing rhymes, you dissolve inwardly towards the institution that is the church; memories hit you and you begin to feel religious. You even join the queue to partake in Holy Communion, even though you have been living in sin with some Ankole girl, back in the city, in which case the bold catechist would have fearlessly pulled you out of the queue, had he known. You resolve to make your peace with God when you go back to Kampala. After mass, you meet some of your peers who chose to marry a local girl rather than proceed to secondary school, calling you a coward who feared women. Now languishing with four children who have to suffered from marasmus followed by kwashiorkor in quick succession without them even noticing, like it was a natural stage of life, selling dry cassava by the roadside, wishing they had not turned down the chance to study, like you.

You realise that your brief adventure in the land of your ancestors is drawing to an end when they cook you, a delicious dish of *ekhubi* - cowpea leaves for which you confess to be craving. Your cousins in the village cannot understand how someone would crave for green leaves soaked and boiled in *magadi*, soda ash, instead of frying it, because they think it is poor people who eat leaves let alone boiled leaves, instead of meat and fish – they just don't understand you. You wolf down the tender leaves with the unique bittersweet taste greedily; knowing the next opportunity you will have to indulge in such a luxury will be the death of another close relative and that of course, would have to be faked. After all, on real funerals, no one has the time to cook leaves. They dedicate all the time to wailing and crying, heartrending songs of loss. You reorganise your beliefs about women; and prepare for another strenuous bus journey back to the artificial noise and chaos of your everyday life in Kampala.

iLOVE
Princess Ikatekit

COMPOSE MAIL

Darling David,

You accuse me all the time of not really opening up to you, especially now that we are trying this long distance thing and have the most awkward phone conversations every other night. You say you do not really *know* me after all this time. I guess I just find it harder to talk about my past than most people. I'm private like that. Perhaps this will finally make you happy. If it seems erratic, it is because my thoughts very often are. You know that already, of course. I think you do, at least. I'll begin at the beginning. I warn you that this might be a very long email. 🙂

There was a hole in the yellow door of my parents' bedroom at our old house. No, there were two holes. But only one was at my eye-level at age 7, so it was the one that I could peek through. It was a rounded hole, about the diameter of the metal pipe that had been driven forcefully through it. I cannot remember the details of how I came to be peeping into the room at that particular time but I tell you, I saw… things. I know now that it was a condom stretched over Uncle Fred's long, black penis as he came out from behind the closet door. Then, I did not know what it was but I remember my cousins laughing when I tried to describe it to them later. I remember, I forgot what I had been sent for. I simply hurried away from the room. But this is not about what I saw through the hole; it is about how those two holes came to be.

My parents must have loved each other in the beginning. My cousins say that my mum turned down a Kenyan businessman to be with my father. They also say that my mother was pregnant with my sister before they were married. Was it my father's heightened sense of responsibility then? I came across some love letters while I was still at home though. My mother had kept them all these years. And in that grainy old wedding tape, they seem genuinely happy. They are both very thin in the video. My father's cheeks are hollowed out such that his forehead stands out in sharp focus and his firm chin is emphasized. His eyes appear to be gaping from his face. He looks like the wind could snap him in half. I much prefer the big, burly man my father is today, so tall and powerful. But his smiles in the video are very radiant; so are my mother's. She was a very beautiful bride. How happy, fairy-tale and forever they look! 🏆 That was way back in 1986.

Ten or so years later, they could not stand each other. When is it that marriages go sour? When do honeyed, dulcet tones turn into dissonant, harsh parodies of what was? I have memories of rather loud arguments, of slamming doors, of Mummy being moved out of the master bedroom, of a certain Aunt Brenda featuring rather regularly in our lives all of a sudden. But the clearest memory by far is of Daddy puncturing that yellow door with those two holes.

The voices were loud, loud! I was peeking from behind my bedroom door, I think. Daddy looked mad, so mad that he seemed to be frothing at the mouth. His face was dark and...formidable. Why was he chasing Mummy? Why was she running? I heard the painful slap as palm connected with skin, and my mother's scream. She ran into their bedroom and slammed the door. Daddy ran outside with a frenzied urgency and returned carrying that heavy metal pipe of a respectable diameter. He rammed the door, hard. I was sure it would shatter from the mere impact, but no, it left the one well-rounded hole. I could hear my mother crying on the other side of the door. He pounded again, and 'TWHACK!' There was the second hole, and the wood splinters on the floor.

I'm afraid the memory goes fuzzy after that part. He must have stopped. Maybe he saw me peeking from my room just down the hall. Maybe he was spent. All I know is, it was over almost as quickly as it had begun. Those two holes in the yellow door were to later become very symbolic to me—each hollowed-out space a reminder of how things on the inside can be… destroyed.

Another memory surges to the forefront of my mind now. It attaches with easy familiarity, because I cannot relive the one without thinking of the other. First, there is the sound of children's running feet slapping the ground. A happy sound! In it is all the carefree laughter and joy that only little feet know how to dance to. Then there is recognition. I think our feet slapped a happy tune when my brother and I ran into the house after school on that all-important afternoon long ago. The driver had just dropped us off, and I remember we barely spared the dusty lorry that was getting ready to leave our compound, a second glance, as we climbed out of the car and ran into the house shouting as loud as we could, 'Mummy! Mummy!'

The house was oddly quiet. My brother and I raced chaotically around all the front rooms, shouting still. If Mummy didn't meet us at the door, she was usually in the kitchen. But we didn't find her there, and when we stopped to listen, we heard nothing. We were subdued as we trooped down the long corridor to her room. Maybe she was sleeping.

We were met with boxes when we opened the door. Great big cardboard boxes piled high with Mummy's things. It was a maze in there! There was a box with only shoes, and another with just handbags. The other boxes were already sealed. Her closet seemed to be laughing at us, with its drawers gaping open and several empty metal hangers wagging like eyebrows. No sign of Mummy. My brother began to cry. You know how it is with kids. First they make annoying whiny sounds, *nyinyinyi*, while their lips start to quiver and their eyes fill up. Then they let rip. Oh, what am I saying? I was doing the same thing.

That's how Daddy found us. His face was solemn when he looked down at our faces.

He said, 'Kids, your mother's gone. She won't be coming back.'

And that's how he left us.

My five year old brother and I wept our hearts out all

afternoon. We drenched our pillows with heaving sobs. Maybe if we cried long enough, Mummy would come back. Maybe if we cried loud enough, Daddy would come and explain. Why did he not explain?

Can I speak plainly, my love? Perhaps there is no better time than the present. You cannot after all cast your unblinking eyes on me, and halt my words mid-phrase. You cannot distract me simply by clasping and unclasping your long, slender fingers; the way you did when you played with the straw-wrapping that last time we had drinks together in Ntinda: fold and press, pull and tear, very slow, your eyes never once leaving mine.

Ai! You distract me even when your face is like a photograph in soft focus—all hazy about the edges, and so irritatingly far out of reach. I want to tell you about the first time I heard the words, 'I love you,' whispered to me. Shush, do not raise your eyebrows at me; listen.

Boarding school for me, is a rapid succession of memories that I push hurriedly to the back of my mind. But as you well know, some memories are too strong to be drowned even by time's overenthusiastic efforts; they surge irreverently to the fore.

Senior 3. I remember the nasty showers we had in our dormitory block. They were always dark, even at 4.30 p.m. when the 3C's dashed from their classes and crowded at the shower doors shouting, 'After you!' to the girls who had managed to triumphantly enter the shower first and sling their towels possessively over the mould-covered doors. The smell of the place! You would think that ladies would consider squatting and allowing urine to splash against their legs and the shower tiles to be *disgusting*, to put it prettily. You would think wrong. It was easy to be stripped of your delusions once you stood in line with your bucket of water and sponge for twenty minutes, while the too generous scent of ammonia wafted all around you, and you finally entered a shower-room to find that its previous occupant had left the bloody evidence of her monthlies lying right there on the floor.

There was a quadrangle which separated the upper block from the lower block. When we had fetched our *posho* and beans from the cafeteria grounds and spiced it with tomato sauce, appetizer and ghee, we would sit in that general area and gossip contentedly in our own cliques. I preferred to sit on the benches that faced out from our block though. There was always the breeze and the relative quiet under the trees. You could watch the sunset over the tea estates a little further down the road from our school, and forget the immediate world, lost in gorgeous reflections.

You know those scars on my legs that I always complain about? Well, they are souvenirs from the box-rooms on S.3 block. I swear their owners placed the jutting edges of their metal tin-boxes just so they could rip into sensitive, unsuspecting skin. There was a time I thought I had more scars on my legs than skin! But the scar on my hand I got from peeling *matooke* on automatic while my eyes followed the Namilyango boys who had come for a social with the S.6's. Boys were a rare delicacy, see, they had to be savoured.

Forgive my dithering; I never could summarise a story, and I don't quite know how to tell this one. I have neither spoken it out loud nor written it down before now.

Ah, where to start? I suppose my dorm room is as good a place as any. Claire and I were in the same dorm. Dorm 3 on upper block. Ours was the only dorm that had just single beds—two rows of twenty or so beds, lined up neatly. It did very nicely. Some of the other dorms were not so lucky though, my but were they cramped! Their rooms boasted of several double-deckers spaced mere inches apart. Jerricans, buckets, slippers and basins took up the rest of the space. It made you wonder if perhaps some politics did not go into the assigning of the dorms because the politics permeated every sphere of our living. Maybe the teachers were aware of it too.

The 3As were the smarts of the Senior Three Class; they aced everything, the nerds! We called them *silent burners* for two reasons: they were quiet, obedient girls who always did as they were told and were always to be found burning their *bitabo* late into the night either in the science labs or in the classrooms, whether it was exam week or not and secondly, a low, slow fire seemed to roast within them, such that they needed only to be provoked to show their true colours, like that time we went on strike in S.4. But that is another story. The Bs were bums;

disrespectful girls who knew how to get through life by doing just the bare minimum. They were the ones who knew how 'to have fun.' And the Cs, they were just crazy. We did not know what to make of them. They oscillated between stark raving mad and loony, at least in our opinions. There was hardly any mixing. That was the way of it. Those were the rules.

Claire was in 3C and I was in 3B. That, plus her bed was on the opposite end of the dorm from mine. No wonder we barely spoke two words to each other till about half-way through our third year's first school term. We had both won the rather dubious honour of, 'Best Article,' that day-- one of the Speech Minister's grander ideas to nudge the school's dying writing culture back to life. The best three writers per class (one from each stream) had to go up on assembly and read their articles to the school. The opportunity for embarrassment abounded! You stood fumbling at the podium in front of the entire school and if you were lucky, maybe they wouldn't snicker too loudly when you began to read. We met to commiserate and to congratulate. I had the most awful stage fright and I thought that Claire's piece was particularly good. Turned out she liked my piece *and* was nervous too. We talked for hours that first night; way past the lights-out bell at 10pm.

But I would say our friendship began two nights later when Claire woke up in a coughing fit and vomited all over the floor next to her bed. I do not know why I was the first to wake and hear her. I do not know why I was not repulsed by the chunks of half-digested food, and the terrible smell. I was on my knees on the floor, mopping it all up, handing her a basin if anything else needed to come up, waiting while she rinsed her mouth out and handing her a glass of water to drink. Was that to be the motif for our friendship? Would we always be cleaning up each other's messes? I did not know nor care; I knew only that a protective instinct had risen up in my chest and I had responded.

You know that you have crossed the boundary between acquaintance and friendship when secrets slip easily from your lips in the other's company. We grew close, Claire and I. We spoke easily about everything under the sun, and sometimes about things — things better disclosed under the cover of darkness. Of these secrets she let me in on; there is one in particular which I cannot quite find a *how* in the telling of.

Do I just blurt out that he periodically whipped out his dick, forced it down her seven year old throat and bade her to suck? Should I mouth it so perhaps you don't hear that he asked her to rub him hard, while he shoved his filthy fingers inside her, and *played* with her? Maybe if I speak really fast you'll miss the part where I tell you he made her shower with him. He pleasured himself and got her to help him. He pinched at her barely formed nipples under the shower stream. He sucked at them; the leeching, fucked up, good-for-nothing...!

She told me his name was Sunday. God sure has a *fucked up* sense of humour, no? He was a cousin visiting from the village too. Claire choked out her story in pieces, and I'll tell you each piece is as vivid in my mind as a jagged-edged mosaic, and each memory of it slices deep. The lying bastard said he'd kill her if she told. It wasn't long till that threat didn't matter though. The shame clamped like an iron hand over her mouth pretty quickly. It hurt sometimes, yes. But there were times she enjoyed it. He said he cared about her, he said he loved her, and he liked to play special, secret games with her. He said so when he was panting over her face. Those were the times she liked it. That couldn't be right, could it? It was bad manners! It was wrong, she was going to hell! How could she tell anyone this shameful thing?

I was the first person that she ever told. Why did she trust me enough? I do not know. Ours was a two week old friendship. I hunched up when she told me. I mean the muscles in my body literally contracted. I must have been growling. Fancy thoughts of me wielding a gun raced through my mind. I dismissed them. It would be far more practical to take Miria Matembe's advice. I would find me some shears and happily go castrate the man!

When Claire burst out crying, I did not know what to do. I patted her awkwardly on the back; my one comforting gesture. My eyes welled up with tears and my mouth said clumsily, 'I would kill him if I ever set eyes on him.' What flat, empty words. I felt...inadequate. But she smiled up at me through her tears, and said, 'Thank you...for not judging me.' Maybe that was all she needed, to have someone there with her, to tell her it wasn't her fault. I could do that. Yes, I could! Slowly, hesitantly, awkwardly, I put my arm around her shoulder. It was like a new beginning.

Later, our classmates would tease that we had become like a couple. We were always together. She was so little that I looked like an elephant next to her. Not a bad comparison when you considered that I had appointed myself her protector. I would keep the big bad world away from her, even if it was the last thing I did.

Some nights were really bad for Claire. Nightmare demons would attack savagely, and she would wake crying, screaming or just in a cold sweat. In S.4, we were assigned to different dorms, and when the nightmares got very bad, she would come over to my dorm after lights-out. Sometimes she stayed the night.

I won't lie. There were days when Claire made me feel like a man. She depended on me. It was such a strange feeling. She would fall apart in my arms and I would hold her. Her pain would be raw, and though I did not cry, my eyes would be wet.

Was it wrong that when her body was wracked with sobs, I held her close and my shirt was drenched with her tears? Was it wrong that once when I held her tight to try and stop her shaking, her lips may have tenderly brushed my forehead? That didn't count as a kiss, did it ⁉️

She slept in my bed some nights when the night demons would not let her be. She said she felt safer that way. Nothing happened. She'd sleep with her feet near my head and I'd place *my* feet near *her* head. She always snuck out before first light too, so the other girls wouldn't see what we'd done. Why did we act guilty?

She whispered, 'I love you,' to me on one of those bad nights. The tears had stopped, and she was hiccupping like a child. She looked right at me and said it. Boy was I stumped! Girls did not say 'I love you,' to girls. These were the facts. Only Americans and lesbians would say such things.

But you know, even if I didn't say anything back that night, I knew that I loved her too. How else could you explain that her pain had become my pain, and her joy was my joy? *If thou sorrow, I shall weep.* I found a couple of my old school journals recently, and in one of them I saw that I had written this poem for her:

I don't want you to cry,
When I'm the cause and why,
I'm the bird who won't fly
If you are not my sky…
What is a Bible without sin?
Or a friendship without trials?
It is an unbalanced equation,
Let us balance the equation.
And get it right, shall we?

I know; how incredibly cheesy! It must have been an apology of sorts. Let's cut to the crux: this then, was what love was. Open, shivering vulnerability. Need for the other person. Caring more about their well-being than your own. Knowing their joy and their sorrow, their strengths and their weaknesses. And accepting them for who they were.

When my parents split up, I cordoned off my heart. I was not willing to believe anymore in a thing that could die; a thing that could end in such bitterness and strife. Claire re-opened my heart to love. What is that Corinthians verse again? 'Love makes no record of wrongs. Love does not judge etc. etc.' She taught me that it is okay to love, yes, even your **girl**friends.

'I love you,' is a commitment forever. I always told myself that the first time I said those words out loud to somebody; I would mean them with my whole heart. You'll be happy to learn that the first time I said those three words out loud, I said them to you. I meant them too. I think.

I started out by telling you that I was letting you in on the *secret* of me. But I have found myself speaking recurrently about love: how I lost it, how I found it. It must be true then what they say, about love being, 'the motor of the world.' Our lives appear to be propelled through their various stages by that beautiful engine, whether we know it or not. I'll write now about the first time I considered myself to be *in* love, happy prisoner of that very intoxicating drug. No, don't turn your face like that. You've told me all about *your* ex-girlfriends. I'm only telling you about one ex-boyfriend. Surely, you can stay your jealousy long enough?

His name was Alan. I was in S.6, and he was a freshman at the

University of Cape Town doing an exotic sounding course. Actuarial Science, I think it was called. We met on one of those flimsy social networking websites: Hi5, I believe. Yes, pre-Facebook. Something about the way I described myself on my profile captured his imagination, he said. I was not like other girls. I was to him as rare as, 'white gold.' For my part, I was intrigued by this stranger, who paid me unique compliments, and had a caustic wit. He was smart too, turns out Ac Sci (that's how he shortened it), is not one of those courses for the feeble-minded. The drop-out rate in his university was through the roof! There's something about an intelligent man that just rocks *my* boat 🔒.

The chatting, sms-ing, and the long emails followed as a matter of course. In fact, he called me after we had exchanged maybe a couple of emails. You know those emails where you try with self-depreciative humour to paint yourself as an unwilling angel or modest genius, and give a run-down of only those parts of your life which you would want people to know about? He did a good job obviously; I did not hesitate with my phone number when he asked for it.

He declared love at the end of our first phone-call. Quick to the thrust, wasn't he? I was amused and very flattered. The idea that just my voice could do things to a boy's heartbeat was... well, appealing. It did wonders for my self-esteem. I could start to like this boy. Yes, I very well could.

They say love makes us do the most stupid things, that our senses, our thoughts, our feelings are plunged into an ever swirling, melting-hot cauldron of passion. What is real is no longer real; our eyes are glazed and begin to look on the world as if everything and everyone therein were a dream, and the object of our love was the only solid feasibility.

I breezed through my Organic Chemistry classes, by which I mean I cupped my face in my hands and watched Mr. Kamanzi write complicated squiggles on the board with a blank smile. And when the mock exams came round and I scored my first F, that was a dream too, I told myself. Real Chemistry was what Alan and I had. I swear my breath caught in my chest when I heard his deep 'Hello' stretch out over the line. The silence on his end when I responded must have been *his* twenty seconds of constricted airway.

Maths Class gave me palpitations. It reminded me of Alan's fascination with numbers and all things finance-related. I could hear his voice in my head; deepening and quickening the way it did whenever he was impassioned about something. The Maths teacher's voice became like a hollow, irritating echo at the back of my head. I got a D in the mock exam. But that was just the teacher's attempt at a joke-- couldn't be real.

Have I told you before about the *namikolo* status I attained at 'A' level? I was Deputy Head Girl, Minister of Speech, President of the Writers' Club, Editor of the school magazine, and biweekly newsletter, Playwright and Play Director of the Drama Club and organiser of numerous social functions. My fingers were in every proverbial pie, which meant I was above reproach—to both the students and the teachers. It was easy to sneak my cell phone into school, and to monopolise the use of the computer lab. I spent most of my prep time at the computers; ostensibly editing articles for the school magazine, but really just exchanging endless love nothings. And late at night, when the silence had grown as heavy as a depressed sigh, I would find the darkest corners in the school from which to answer his calls. I always giggled when I found that the darkest corner on one night or another was in the secret garden next to the convent. Ah, the thrill of danger! What if Sister Headmistress were to look up from her rosary reciting and spot me through her window? I was almost caught by an *askari* one night, but they were always easy to pay off, if you played your cards right. Heck, they were the ones who bought us the airtime!

Call me cynical, but I believe that a guy's not really into a relationship until he feels that he has an absolute hold on the girl; when he has been able to *teach* her something, when he has convinced himself that she would be worse off without him, when he has been able to show up on a horse and whisk her away from any would-be dangers. And a girl, she is not really into a relationship until she feels she has arms she can run into, to feel warm, and loved and *protected*. The dawning of clarity is like ice cold water thrown unexpectedly over your naked back. It jerks you wide-awake with a gasp. Alan was cold, clinical and calculating. I think he viewed the world through measured eyes:

what is there to be gained from this person or thing? Are they useful to me still? I knew this, but I had decided long before to treat his character flaws as a blessing. They made him far more practical, and he never told a lie. He was blunt to the point of callousness, which was a good thing, right? I was in his good books after-all. And then suddenly, I wasn't. Perhaps I gushed too much about how he made me feel. See, we talked about everything and anything that crossed our minds. In retrospect, I can see when it was that my over-eagerness started to push him away. But I didn't see it then. He called me at the beginning of my second term holidays, and I answered as usual with breathless excitement.

'We need to talk.'

'Why so serious?' I laughed.

I soon found out why. These are snippets from my school journal about what he said:

'I need my space…'

'You must have realised I use my head more than you do…'

'Your insecurities…'

'I love you, I do but…'

'I'd rather hurt you now in the short term rather than in the long term.'

Pain. The fire stung at the back of my eyes, burned its way to my chest and squeezed at the seemingly dead blood pumping device. The whole of me all but stopped. I wanted to beg and plead with him, to sway that cold logic of his. But then the pride kicked in, and in a maniacal haze I hang up, and deliberately deleted all evidence of him from my phone. I would purge myself.

'I am the devil come to steal your peace.' It sounded… sexy the first time he said that to me. Now the words danced mockingly before my eyes.

I was numb, and disbelieving. It struck me as ironic that my first attempt at love for a member of the male sex—'Love' in the purely sensual sense of the word should prove my reasons for every other aborted attempt to be true.

You say that you have never had your heart broken, for the simple reason that you were never in love *until* me. Let me describe the feeling to you.

First the questions and the doubts crowd your mind. What did I do wrong? Is there anything the matter with me? Am I ugly? 😭 Was what we had real? Where and when did we veer off-track? Did I fall short of some stupid ideal? Actually, for me the answer to the last question would be yes. Alan was a graphology buff. Graphology is the study and analysis of handwriting in relation to human psychology. Supposedly you can determine a person's character and behavioural traits from the slant of their handwriting and the pressure of their pen on paper.

He told me later that I crossed my *t*'s too low. That was why we would never work out. He broke up with me because a dumb-ass textbook told him I crossed my *t*'s too low and high *t* bars and low *t* bars could never survive in a long-term relationship.

Total FML. But I digress.

What overwhelms your being next is the denial. It can't have happened. He *loves* me. This is all a very bad joke. I love him so much, can't he see that? He has to be able to see that. I will *make* him see that. There follows the embarrassing begging. 'Take me back, please take me back!' Was I above the begging? Afraid not! I insist mine was a rather dignified begging though. I sent him a three-word text that read:

'I miss you' .

His response: **'You' ll get over me soon enough. '**

People deal with rejection in different ways. They binge on food, they drink themselves silly, and they have sex with random strangers. You feel used, discarded, vulnerable and ashamed. At least, I did. I wrote frantically and furiously; determined not to shed a tear over the bastard. Oh, but I came close. Those days were dark. Corny love songs started to make sense. Sometimes the sun decided to skip coming out altogether. I poured my grief into studying for the UNEB finals. I found God again .

Three months. That's how long it took for me to get over him. I am afraid even now to reconnect with the horror of those few months to describe it to you. I knew desperation, loss of self, hopelessness, bitterness. The pain I felt can be compared to the pain an amputee feels in the place where his missing limb ought to be. It's funny when you think about it: how could my heart break over a disembodied voice? There were no physical reminders, no kisses, no warm hugs, no frantic gropings in dark corners, no favourite smells even! How is it that I managed to pull fantastic happy memories of him from my mind?

You know, David; I scare myself sometimes. If I could hurt so much over a relationship which really was no more than a meeting of the minds and a healthy dose of imagination, what would happen to me in a real relationship? A relationship where proximity would mean hot breaths mingling? Alan is a big part of the reason why you feel you cannot get through to me. I grew these protective walls as a forceful healing mechanism. You understand that, don't you?

It was easy to rebuff guys in the nine or so months following Alan. Easy that is, until there was you. You with your skinny frame, impish lop-sided half-smile, quirky little swagger and eyes that crinkled at the corners. You have that rather annoying habit of knowing when I am bull-shitting too 😕 .

I remember the last Lantern Meet of The Poets that we attended together. The week before you had asked me to meet you at Mateo's, and sitting across the table from me, gripping my hands tightly and forcing me to look at you, you had laid your cards on the table.

'I want you,' you had said. I had been too flustered to reply.

Now here we were, walking away from the National Theatre; just the two of us. I was riding on the intellectual high, which comes from reading and critiquing really beautiful poetry, but I was not too blind to feel the tension which twanged in the air, as taut as a newly tightened guitar string. I knew you still wanted your answer. Did we walk down Parliamentary Avenue? I think we did. All I can remember clearly though is that semi-dark alley where you pushed me up against the wall, leaned your forehead against mine and said slowly so I wouldn't doubt you, 'G, I love you.' I remember panicking and wishing frenziedly that you would take your stupid confessions back so we could return to being just good friends.

Then there was that night when you walked me home, and we hugged goodbye. At least, it started out as a hug. You began to rub at my back, and your hands slipped lower, and lower. You dared to squeeze my butt and I did not stop you. You dared to kiss me, long and deep; I did not resist. My hands roamed carelessly, and found their way into your trousers. You did not stop me, even when it became necessary for you to grab at the nearby wall for support.

Do I love you, or merely lust after you then? I do not know. Who am I to even pretend to understand love or its mechanics? All I know is that I will be very eager to see you come August. This long distance business will kill me!

Sigh. I have tried but I cannot hit 'send'. I think I'll just save this to 'drafts'. I'm not quite ready to hand you all of my heart on a… cyber platter. What I meant to send you originally will do.

 COMPOSE MAIL

Hi Love, I miss you. I've been really busy with schoolwork and everything. How are you? Do write soon and tell all.

Love you, G.

SEND

1 4 THE RD ... TILL 4 AM
Jackee Budesta Batanda

Lumu finds out in their final year that Namaqua has been two-timing him with their Communication Skills lecturer. They have been an item for three years. Three years, he believes he is dating an angel, until a little bird whispers something in his ear. He regrets for the umpteenth time, listening to the rumours. Lumu wishes it were a fib, then he wouldn't be sitting alone in *1 4 the Rd...till 4 am*, a makeshift bar in Wandegeya on a bloody Friday evening, downing Bell Lager after Bell Lager, despondent tears rolling down his cheeks, contemplating confronting the slithery bastard and stabbing him, or better still killing his miserable fucking self.

The tears taste salty on his tongue. Some drop in his glass as he listens to some crap Ugandan musician hollering truncated gibberish through the ancient speakers, that, he's sure, have seen better times, perhaps in the 70s; and calling it a song. Where the hell do producers get these amateurish chaps? And why do bar owners buy the low-cost tapes, and play them loudly, especially when they have customers as blue as he is anyway? Lumu muses. He tries to shout to the flabby waitress wearing a tight, low-neck black blouse, pushing her breasts out so that they look like oranges about to drop, walking cautiously in the extremely blue dim lighting, dodging the groping hands of drunken patrons grabbing her ass held firmly in equally tight, red leather pants. Most of these little squalid bars around Wandegeya have this grand idea of using cheap coloured bulbs in an attempt to create a romantic atmosphere for the poor drunks that frequent them, squandering their meagre money, before heading home to their equally squalid homes.

Under the light, Lumu can't make out whether she is a beauty or not. His voice slurs, drowned out by the deafening gibberish from the speaker, and he bangs the low wooden table before him, whose light green paint is peeling off, revealing inferior wood underneath.

Lumu could have let the regrettable incident pass, if Namaqua had cheated on him once, like we all have in our moments of weakness, but three years has encompassed too many times for him to forgive. It makes him feel like a rickety Fuso truck has run over him.

He is unsure whether it is anger or embarrassment that makes him seek this drab bar, with beads hanging in the doorway and dim lights, to sit with these low lives like he is one of them. He chases off the vendors that come shoving roast pork on wooden skewers sandwiched between two white plastic plates, asking him to buy the 'tasty muchomo' under his nose. He doesn't want anything in his body but the booze, which he will have in plenty. His mind has turned riotous as he remembers that his heart has been broken. Someone once told him that when your heart breaks; it's like an egg cracked at the top which cannot be mended. Right now, he is that egg without a top.

Because Lumu keeps buying beer after beer, the waitress manages to remit smiles his way. He only nods. His mind draws to the Communication Skills lecturer; a fifty something guy, with drooping lips, eyes so big that they give him a froglike appearance, and greying hair he relentlessly dyes, leaving his hairline with a pale brown tint. He always wears tie-dye shirts over the same pair of pants and sometimes, outrageous oversized flowery silk shirts. He swears the guy has such awful style. And he sees his angelic Namaqua, with him, moaning in ecstasy as he thrusts his shrivelled penis in her. Ugggh!!! How could she do this to him? He moans as he takes another swig at his drink. The bar empties of patrons, but he keeps at his table. This place is renowned for closing with the last customer. This evening the waitress is not willing to wait for this gloomy customer in the corner to leave. She has other plans on her mind. She has watched him the whole evening ordering beer after beer and has decided he will be a good catch for the night. Probably he will have something extra in his wallet she will nick at the end of the mind-blowing sex session she has in mind for him.

At 2 am, the waitress starts clearing the litter left behind by the other customers.

'I will see this customer out,' she tells the cashier, 'you can leave now. I will lock up.' She winks at him. He understands. He locks the safe and ambles out through the backdoor. She saunters to the client and coos, 'Sir, I am going to close the bar.'

Lumu nods and says, 'I waaant annozzer beer, and zis bar closez wiz the last customer. I have my money,' he slurs.

She whispers, 'I know a place, where you can get free beer.'

Her voice sounds musical. He looks up at her and meets her smiling face. And when you have had a dozen beers, even a toad will look like Halle Berry. She holds out her hand to him. And at that moment, he feels like he is being led to heaven. He struggles to get up and she bends over to help him, carrying his weight. She leads him to the door as he strives to regain his balance. He leans against the wall, holding a half empty bottle of Bell Lager. She gets a bunch of keys and locks the door. Together, they stagger on the slippery murram road, dodging heaps of shit and food remains strewn on the path. Most of the bars have closed and the music has died down. Lumu swings his bottle as he croons Steve Jean's *Osobolyotya*, another quack song moaning about a betrayed love; whatever. Suddenly he stands still in his tracks, gives her the bottle and ambles to a trench filled with sewage, and probably polythene bags, bottles and papers. He unzips his pants and pisses into the trench; the stench of urine rising in the air. He walks back, snatches the bottle, takes the last draught, and then throws it on the ground. He laughs at her stunned expression in the moonlight. She nods suspiciously, grabs him and continues. They move deeper into the slum, jumping over numerous puddles, which litter the place like ringworms. The tenement houses here lean on each other like moaning trees swayed by a strong wind. They get to the end of the block. She retrieves a key from her bra and opens the creaking wooden door, pushing away the flimsy door net. He staggers up the broken steps into the room. He looks around trying to focus his eyes in the dark.

'It's not load shedding,' she whispers, 'the UEB guys disconnected our power line saying it was illegal. I will light a candle.'

She makes her way through the darkness, knocking down saucepans in the process, which make clanking sounds as they spin and finally settle on the floor. She manages to locate the matchstick and candle. The flame dances mournfully like the shabby room that stands before him. The unpainted wall covered with newspaper cuttings of local pop stars is overly crowded. Her portrait is captured in a slanting faded gold frame hanging on a loose nail with a blue knitting thread holding it in place. Suspended beside it is a poster with the words, 'Christ is the Head of this house.'

She pulls Lumu to the bed standing solemnly in the corner, behind a torn flowery curtain.

Later, he mourns on her sweaty bosom, telling her how his Namaqua has mercilessly ripped his heart out. His heart, he says, has passed through a paper shredding machine. He wonders when Namaqua changed. When it started. When she lost her innocence. Makerere University, he knows deflowers many girls of their innocence and turns them into up-class call girls. It is a place where heaven and hell meet. He was sure his girl would withstand the temptations that lure many 'good' girls… The words splatter out of his mouth and drop like rain on dry ground, splashing a little here and there. She had not planned for a night of calming a man whose heart has been shredded into pieces of paper. But she holds him in her arms and coos in his ears, covering him with kisses. Her hand trails slowly down his warm, clammy back trying to find that sensitive point she can soothe to make him sleep so she can go through his wallet. But sleep is the last thing on his mind, as he unburdens his heart, discarding his load on her, for her to ponder the next few years, wondering why any sane girl would two-time a guy like him.

But she understands what Makerere does to students fresh from A levels. It turns their heads round like it turned hers. It always starts with a girl who knows someone who knows someone who knows someone who can provide a wild night of fun at no cost.

Then the partying begins; clubbing every night, sneaking back in the halls, jumping over the gate, which the warden has locked and climbing through windows to catch a few hours of sleep before attending lectures and the clubbing resuming. If it is not the guy who takes you partying asking for sex then it's the lecturer. It starts with one piece of coursework not being returned and on enquiring why it is missing; he pulls it out from the scattered pile on his desk and warns that if a relationship does not start immediately, then more coursework will go missing and missing coursework means failing exams and having the hideous word RETAKE reflected on the transcript. It is a win-lose thing. No way round it. So start stolen moments of raucous sex on the office desk, sometimes over piles of coursework, sometimes, getting more daring; tempting fate and doing it in the afternoon.

She listens to him sob about how he spent a semester's tuition taking his girl to the most expensive places in town from Andy the Greek, to La Fontaine Restaurant, to the Sheraton Hotel, Sabrina's Pub, Speke Resort Munyonyo, you name it. He says, 'My girl deserved the best and I was willing to stake my education for her.' He almost misses his second year examinations because he has splashed the money on her until someone says he can get him out of the filthy mess. He has a contact. Tycoon. Everyone calls him Tycoon because he keeps the cash rolling. Well… if you are interested.

*

The meeting takes place at CLUB 5 between the Faculty of Law and Complex Hall. Over mineral water, like they are straight guys, or poor students ill-affording anything else and resorting to water to pass the afternoon, the recruit is made. Tycoon has, 'a special clientele who demand for the best Kampala had to offer. And Makerere University is the home of the best.'

He looks at Tycoon perplexed.

'I don't understand you,' he says, irritated that instead of talking about money, Tycoon is wasting his time. Because he is in a tight spot, he listens like the most interested party on earth.

Tycoon explains 'Like this mineral water we are drinking now, people want it and someone delivers it here to meet the demand of customers…'

'I am not following you, where do I come in?'

Tycoon watches him silently before resuming, speaking very slowly like he is speaking to a child. 'What I am saying is I have a list of men with big bucks, who want a wild night with pretty little things that the university is teeming with. So I need someone to deliver the goods. You get paid after each delivery, so it is how smooth you operate. Of course, I will give you an allowance to create an image. You get what I'm saying?' he asks his bewildered listener.

'Uhmm…I have to think about this…' he manages.

'Time is our enemy at the moment. Forget about the morals, we all know Makerere girls are call girls. If you don't do it, someone else will and you will still miss your exams, because you spent your money on a little girl?.'

Before Tycoon walks away to his BMW, he gives Lumu thirty thousand shillings and adds, 'do think about it.' His perfume lingers at the table and leaves a bewildered boy thirty thousand richer.

A day to exams, he pays his tuition. That is his entry into the pimping business; connecting campus girls to clients ranging from expatriates, diplomats to rich men around town and sometimes the university lecturers. The first time he delivers a girl to a lecturer he knows, both avoid each other's eyes. The next time he meets the lecturer along the Faculty of Arts gardens, the lecturer tells him, 'this is life, you know that?' He nods.

That is how he is able to maintain his lifestyle and give Namaqua the best. It is easy recruiting the girls – promises of a handsome income over a glass of Amarula or V&A sherry at *The Venue* and guarantees of success do the trick. For most he says, 'the clients are a gateway to your wildest dreams,' and they do have wild dreams. Sometimes, he admits, he sleeps with them before connecting them to clients. His Namaqua isn't like any of the call girls he traded – they come with a variety of business names Candy, Sunshine, and Island…

Namaqua is not a professional call girl. She is different…

*

When Lumu finally sleeps, exhausted by his confession, she lies listening to his slow breathing with the night turning into day. Her past has come back to her with this man barely sliding into sleep. Once she had been like his Namaqua.

She moves slowly, careful not to awaken him. Reaching for his pants on the cement floor, she searches for his wallet. Getting it out, she stands up, draws the curtain back and lights another candle. She scatters the contents of the wallet, out falls a passport size picture of a girl, who looks innocently at the camera, like she believes the world is a safe place, and that girls truly come to Makerere to get a decent education. She remembers the guy saying something about having met his girl in church. She looks like the little girls, who were always chosen to be Mary in the Sunday school Christmas plays. You know those little girls, with round faces, innocent eyes and extremely light skinned. Then she knows that this girl has not been corrupted by the contacts of someone who knows someone who knows someone who will provide them with a wild night of fun at no cost. Rather it is the latter; the lecturer summons her to his office for missing coursework and lays his intentions flat in her surprised face, while she tries to make sense of what the man is telling her. She probably wrings her hands in discomfort and says she will think about it. She has seriously thought about it when perhaps, she and her man flunk that particular paper and she makes up her mind, to meet this lecturer's demands if she and her man are to complete the course in a span of three years. She had not bet on her man finding out. And she has done well for herself, going on for three years.

She puts the picture back in the wallet and takes out some money. She counts the money; it is the reason she has brought the man lying in her bed now like it is his, for payment of the wild night of ecstasy she has provided.

LIVING HOPE
Glaydah Namukasa

Kato stares at the long stretch of spear grass ahead. Far beyond, the field extends towards the forest. He imagines himself wrapped up in the security of the bramble thicket which makes up the forest undergrowth. That place, where light switches to darkness, will shut him away from the cruel guards.

Tinkles fill the air as hoes hit stones buried in the ground. The noise is unending because the ground is hard. Gradually, one by one the weary prisoners will faint and they will be dragged into the shade. Occasionally, a prisoner or two will die, but work will still continue, and an unbent back will still call for a whip from the guards. But for this moment, Kato has to keep himself unbent because it is only in this position that he can scrutinise his promising haven.

He turns to look back. The nearby armed guard is seated on a tree stump, the handle of his rifle touching his booted feet. He is poised, ready to shoot any prisoner venturing to escape. The other three guards are at the far side of the field engrossed in raucous laughter. Kato turns and casts a furtive glance at his hoe blade. The stone, his weapon to freedom, is secure.

'You!' The guard snaps.

Oh no! The guard has already noticed his straight back. Over his shoulder, he sees the guard sauntering towards him. The bowlegs. The protruding stomach threatening to push through the miss-buttoned grey shirt. The grim face heating with overt fury as if to burn the worn-out sisal hat.

'The rest continue digging, I am talking to this fool,' the guard shouts.

Kato swoops down, snatches the stone and aims at the guard's forehead. He dashes. Thorns pierce his feet and worsen the existing wounds. The grass cuts across his face and bare torso but he has to get away. He can't be caught, never again. He is going home to his wife – and his child. The child he has never seen.

Gunshots ricochet, mingling with the chorus of voices. Gunpowder pollutes the air, but Kato smells home. He smells fish smoking on his homemade fireplace. He smells the distinctive aroma of brewed *tonto.*

Noises: pursuing footsteps, bullets piercing through the elephant grass, heading for his head or chest. He has to outdo the bullets, outdo light, time – yes time. Time runs fast – so it is said, but he has to disprove the saying. If time runs fast, why have the ten years in prison felt like centuries? He has to beat his wings hard and leap into space, soar into the sky like an eagle. He has to get away!

The hedge unfolds ahead of him, rising higher as he approaches. He takes a stance and hauls his body in the air. His right leg entangles in the hedge top. As the left leg follows, he charges down the band of thick shrubs. A tingle grabs his left thigh. His foot lands on a broken bottle piece. Blood spurts from the punctured thigh. It flows along his leg and mingles with that from the sole of his foot.

He struggles on. It's a long time since he ever felt physical pain. The years in prison have transformed his body into a log. Now he is immune to physical pain. It's the psychological pain he is left with: the agony of missing his wife – and child; the indignation of his unfair imprisonment, the gloom of living the life of a yokeless shell, despised even by a fly. That pain which has held tenaciously and ripped his heart apart day by day. That pain which has for ten years confined him to misery. Now, what is physical pain which comes and goes?

The late evening sun welcomes him to his harbour. He's lost his pursuers. When, and where, he cannot tell. He approaches a fallen *muvule* trunk and sits down on the low end. He looks down at the wound on his thigh; it's a deep wound, the blood is congealed and dark but it will heal. Physical wounds always heal. All the scars on his legs, face, and back were once wounds, some of them as wide as the unending heavens and others as deep as boreholes. Scars: results of daily battering and assault. These scars always stir flames of anger in his heart; anger which heats up and transforms his heart into rock. But this rock heart cracks when he thinks of Edna. Like now; is she still single? Will she accept him – love him again?

Kato jolts up, gathers his torn khaki shirt and then clutches it around himself. Edna is waiting for him, and he must get to her! He moves on with a determination that overpowers tiredness. Spiky *Kawule* shrubs worsen his tattered khaki shorts. He tears off the lower part of the short to mid-thigh level. The night walk is peaceful because he is going home. It's safe too because wild animals are better than people. If you do not bother them, they do not bother you. If they are satisfied they do not bother you. They have spent the whole day hunting so they cannot be hungry. Besides, animals are friendly and fair. The enemy is a fellow human being, man!

The voice of the dusking forest is so sharp in his ears: chirping crickets and croaking frogs, monkeys jumping on and off trees – saying goodnight to each other – and to him perhaps. As he struggles on, he stumbles over a wandering root and swoons down, face first. He rolls on to his back and lays still. He can't go on.

*

The early morning breeze streams through the treetops, humming a tune for the leaves. The dancing leaves perspire, sending beads of sweat to the ground. A droplet spatters on Kato's forehead. He rises, jerking his back off the ground as if he has just been bitten by a gnat. Is it moonlight? Daylight? More droplets spatter on his body, washing the flash of illusion off his eyes. He smells a fresh scent of rotten leaves, bird and monkey droplets, and tree sap: the animating scent of freedom. A fragrance that makes him forget the ghastly odour of the cell. He sits up and looks at the ashen skin of his scarred arms and legs. It's covered with clotted blood, dust and humus. His feet are sore. His stomach is rumbling. But it is all right; after all he is going home.

A sudden noise cuts through the silence. Kato places his palms behind his ears and listens; pounding footsteps, breaking sticks, and voices! Panic jolts through his body. It grows to fear. Fear grows to terror. He creeps backwards and crawls into the thick undergrowth. He lies flat and presses his body against the soft earth. Something under his stomach prods him: a stone perhaps. But it's okay. Physical pain doesn't last long.

The noise gets louder, footsteps nearer. The rustle through the shrubs intensifies. Two of the guards have taken to the direction of his hideout. What slices through his heart is the fact that they halt near his hiding place. One of them, famous among the inmates for his bald head, is facing the thicket. The other, famous for his long legs is facing away; they are so close that he can smell their familiar odour, a mixture of stale cigarettes, tobacco, urine, sweat, alcohol. He, too, smells that unmistakable stench of the bucket in the inner room of the cell.

'We must find him!' The finality of baldhead's words is etched in his red eyes. 'I still can't understand how this happened. I had strict orders on Kato since his forth attempt at escape.'

'He stoned the guard,' long legs says.

'But there were many guards on duty!'

'It was a mess, Afande. Some of the prisoners tried to escape, but we all did our best.'

'But Kato escaped.'

'I did my best, Afande. I chased him, I even tried to shoot him, but the man —'

'But the man did what, dodged the bullets? Do you know the extent of the risk we stand now? We lose our jobs, or we get arrested...' A chesty cough interrupts his speech. He coughs so hard that his shoulders shake as if he's having a fit. He later spits. Some of the sputum messes up his shirt buttons. He seems not to have noticed as he takes a step closer towards long legs and says, 'Find him!'

'I think we should alert the village locals, especially around this area where the forest connects to the swamp. I know many are already in their gardens.'

'Sweep the forest. Shake it till he drops to the ground.'

Under the shrubs, Kato is just a piece of ghee in a heating saucepan. He feels as if the shrubs are opening their mouths to talk, to give him over to bald head. Every leaf and stick above is mocking him, telling him they are jumping away any second. That he was a fool to trust their safety. He squeezes his eyes shut to stifle the welling tears because if they flow, they will carry away hope of seeing his wife – and child. He waits for the two to either sweep his hiding place or move away, but when he opens his eyes, he sees long legs hurrying forward.

Baldhead takes a few steps forward then halts. Suddenly, he jumps back, drops the gun and then fidgets to pull off his trousers. Ants!

Kato steals up. Luck is on his side. And since luck isn't static, he has to act immediately. Ants have opened the door. He reaches for the stone under him and aims at bald head. Bald head makes a guttural sound as he thuds down.

Kato darts forward and grabs the gun. He points the nozzle at bald head. 'You move I shoot.' He is trembling. He has lived with guns for ten years but he has never touched one. And he hates these commanding machines. On the many occasions its nozzle has faced him, he's frozen. He's had to die to his desires, especially the desire of escape; and live for whatever the gun commanded. He's afraid he can touch the trigger and kill bald head or kill himself or even alert the rest of his pursuers.

As he stands irresolute with the gun, he notices that bald head is already unconscious. He drops it and dashes. This time he is saying goodbye to his pursuers. He extends his thanks to the forest for being a fair haven. He thanks the birds, snakes, monkeys, worms and all the forest inhabitants as well as trees for loving him; for supporting his cause.

Noises mingle with the continuous croaks in the swamp: the chorus of yells of children cheering a fast runner, and the shriek of hungry pigs. Kato approaches a field of maize and plucks a shoot of maize corn. He peels it. The grains have barely grown. He steals into a field of flowering coffee plants. His home village is still very far away, but looking at these gardens brings hope to his heart.

*

Night has taken on its duty. The moon is full. Mosquitoes bob and swish, some trying to stick their teeth into Kato's skin. He is heading for what he knew as the tree-hedged path that led to the football field adjacent to his home. The journey is over. He scrambled over rocks, took paths in bushes to avoid any prying eyes, walked uphill and downhill; now he is home! He imagines himself at home, knocking on the door, Edna waking up and asking who it is in a low voice – soft and smooth. Edna's voice is soft and smooth. What will he say that won't frighten her? Edna will open the door, and – his child will be clinging to her skirt. Edna will reach for the kerosene lamp and scrutinise his face. She will blink her eyes to make sure what she is seeing is real...

The imaginations widen the smile hovering on Kato's lips. He hurries forward but the tree-hedged path he is heading for does not appear. The road is deserted. He had expected people to be moving any hour of the night because this is a new government: the government of freedom – or so he heard. He halts in his steps, turns to look back and then forwards. There is no mistake; this is the way to his home. But where were the coffee plants and the banana plantations which were supposed to be surrounding the mud-and-wattle houses? Where were the large compounds where coffee was supposed to be spread for drying?

He dashes forward, through the football field, past the low set wide house which he recognises as Mzee Mukasa's house; he stops at the site of his own home. What once was his home is now a dilapidated building surrounded by overgrown weeds. The house has no roof. This house which took him three years of hard work to build is supposed to be a mud-and-brick house with wooden doors and windows! It is supposed to be Edna's house! Where is his bride Edna? Where is his child? Or is he lost? Anyone could get lost, especially after ten years of being cut off from normal life. Anyone, but not him; the picture of it all is still fresh in his mind. Right here at the edge of what was his compound, is where the army vehicle found him...

That night Edna started feeling premature labour pains accompanied by bleeding.

'Relax my dear, I am going to borrow a bicycle from Mzee Mukasa and rush you to hospital.' Kato said, and rushed out of the house. A sudden flash of car lights blinded his eyes. 'Sumama!' a voice said. Two solders jumped off the vehicle; one held his arms towards his back while the other blindfolded him. The first blow landed in his ribs. He jerked to a crouch, ducking from the second blow, which was aimed at his stomach. He fell down. More blows rained on his head. Every word of plea, every wince of pain called for more blows. When the beatings stopped, two hands pulled him up into a vehicle. They drove off…

Kato pats his forehead to dispel the haunting memories. He turns back and drags his feet into Mzee Mukasa's compound. He knocks on the door.

'It's me, Kato. Mzee Mukasa, please open for me.'

The door opens. Mzee is holding a kerosene lamp forward; his eyes squinting as he tries to scrutinize the face of the late night visitor.

'It's Kato. I am back.' He takes a step inside. The light of the flickering lamp casts a shadow across Mzee's wrinkled face. The old man seems to be either dumb or deaf or even blind. 'I am your neigh… was your neighbour.'

'Kato?' Mzee whispers. 'Kato is dead. He was killed ten… he disappeared—'

'I didn't die.'

'Kato?' Mzee says but his voice is still a whisper. He places the lamp on the floor and opens the door wide. He steps aside and watches Kato enter.

Kato moves slowly and takes the offered seat in an upholstered armchair: the only chair in the room. This house used to be full of chairs, full of children, full of noise, and full of food especially fish, sweet potatoes, *matooke*, and yams. Right now Mzee's wife and grandchildren would have been hurrying out of their bedrooms to see the late night visitor. 'Are you alone in the house, Mzee?'

Mzee stares at him for a long time. Without a word, he disappears into the next room and returns with a shirt. 'You must be cold.'

'But I am not, Mzee.' It's hard for such blood, violated as his has been, to feel cold. Ten years of chilly mornings left his once warm blood inured to coldness. And what's more, these scars etched on his body took away the skin's sensations. But cold or not, the real issue was that it was not worth Mzee's shirt touching his filth.

'I am so much used to being without a shirt,' Kato adds but he does not resist when Mzee drapes the shirt over his shoulders. He clutches on to it.

It is silent, each is listening to the other's breath. Kato hates such silence because it liberates the noises in his head. He especially hates the echoes of the chesty coughs which always filled the cell at night. Mzee disappears into the room again and returns with a plastic cup. Kato notices that both Mzee's hands are shaking terribly and the water in the cup is pouring on his bare feet.

'Drink this water.'

'Thank you, Mzee.' Kato receives the cup in both hands. It's not that he really needs this water; he is just glad to be here. This scent of freedom is so alive and fresh like newly cut grass on a drizzling morning. Receiving this cup from Mzee makes him feel loved. And being loved cements his hope of Edna's existence.

'My wife…' he starts, then pauses to read the expression on Mzee's face. The flickering glow of the kerosene lamp only highlights Mzee's carefully arranged look of surprise and disbelief. Suddenly, Mzee turns his back once again, reaches for the Kerosene lamp, and disappears back into the same room.

Kato feels weak. For ten years he has lived to make his heart believe Edna and the child are alive. But now, this moment, a moment so close to the truth only serves to highlight his insidious anxiety. He forces the cup to his lips and takes a sip. The water chokes him, and he places the cup down.

The approaching patch of light tells him Mzee is back in the room. Slowly he lifts his face and finds that Mzee is walking towards him with a plate of food. He rises off his seat and takes the plate from Mzee's hands. He says, 'I will eat, Mzee, but please tell me, is my wife… is my wife - '

'Your wife is fine, and your son too.'

'My son?' Kato places the plate of food down on the floor. He falls on to his knees and says, 'thank you, Mzee Mukasa.' He then sits back into the chair and reaches for the food. Ten years ago, this would have been fish with either potatoes or *matooke*. Now it's a mixture of half-cooked beans and cassava. If food changed with the change of government, then the government changed for the worst. Kato notices that Mzee is still standing and watching him. 'You still can't believe I am the one, Mzee. It's me, Kato, and you've just brought life back into my wasted body. My wife and son are alive, not so Mzee? You've just told me so.' He talks between mouthfuls.

'Yes I have.'

'Please sit down, Mzee.' Kato leaves the upholstered chair and instead sits down on the floor.

'I should sit down but I can't,' Mzee says. 'I want to know what happened to you, where you have been, why... how... I don't know what to ask you first, Kato.'

'Are you alone here?'

'My wife died. My children got married and left home. I live with two of my grandchildren but they are asleep.'

'I am sorry for your wife.'

'Eat. Finish that food. You need it.'

Kato picks a piece of cassava and nibbles on it. He later says, 'Take the seat, Mzee. I am more comfortable here on the floor.'

'I'll take the seat; you eat and finish up the food.'

'And my wife?'

'Eat, Kato. Finish the food.'

'I left her helpless, Mzee. She was bleeding.'

'She is a brave woman. She walked up to my house soaked in blood. My wife helped her. The baby was premature, but my wife knew what to do. The baby survived. They both survived.'

Kato knows he should either be jumping or crying for joy, but he is just nibbling at the food. He is still searching every angle for an explanation for the cause of his fate.

'That night, I was coming to your house to borrow a bicycle to take Edna to hospital. I was kidnapped, blindfolded, and tortured... does she think I abandoned her?'

'I haven't said that, Kato, and no one ever said you abandoned her.'

'So then does she still love me?'

'How can I answer that?'

'Well then, just tell me, is she still single?'

After a long, heart-suspending silence in which Mzee refuses to answer his question, Kato places his half full plate of food down. He continues, 'I was blind folded, I don't know for how long. The next time I was able to open my eyes and see clearly, two naked men were lying next to me. First I heard a chesty cough escape from one corner. It sparked off multiple coughs. The atmosphere smelt of stale cigarettes, tobacco, urine, sweat – and yes, I was already a prisoner! Why, Mzee, why?'

'I wish I had a valid answer to your question.' Mzee finally talks. 'Those were times when all questions remained hanging on our lips.'

'Why?' Kato whispers to himself. He wonders if the blazing flame in his heart will ever cool down. This is not desperation; neither can he term it as mere anger. It hits him, whirling in his heart like a possessed cloud of dust. Even in this absence of an answer, he still can't call himself a victim of those times. Times when once one was a soldier, then one could make orders and those orders had to be obeyed without question. A soldier could come to your house, command you to pack all your belongings and then carry them to wherever he wished them to be carried. Those times: times when one could be forced to hold down the legs of your own wife or daughter for a group of rapist soldiers. Times of the rowdy army! Kato wonders who to blame for those times; the president, no doubt: a president who had no idea an army needed control. A president whose regime only aimed at hurting the common man: like him, a farmer, a groom who had only known the happiness of marriage for one year, a man who was yet to hold the child of his own, in the strength of his arms.

'I never hurt anyone, Mzee, I wasn't even involved in any political parties! I was just a farmer.'

'It was a disastrous time, Kato. A time of great instability, insecurity, undisciplined army—'

'Still, that doesn't explain why I was captured.'

'I am not trying to explain why you were captured. I am trying to remind you of that time when law and order was a component of the blowing wind.'

'I had done nothing wrong.'

'Don't torture yourself, anymore. There is only one word that can explain your fate. Curfew! You were found outside after eight in the night! That is the crime you committed.'

'A crime I committed?'

'Yes. You broke the curfew rule.'

'Well then I needed a trial. I needed to defend myself in court. I broke a curfew rule as you've said, but I had good cause. Anyone would have done anything to save the life of his wife – and child!'

'Yes, you deserved a trial,' Mzee says.

'And then the government changed. And we heard it had changed for the best so I waited.' Day by day Kato waited to see 'the best' in the change of government. But the days of waiting lagged on, leaving behind snail marks of hopelessness. Some prisoners were killed, others released. Some of the political detainees were released, and others killed.

'I remained in prison; no one came to visit me.'

'No one knew you still lived, Kato. Six months after your disappearance bones were discovered by the bank of river Kasanje at the junction where the river meanders down to the Kasanje forest. Word went around that it was the work of the army. And as you know, if such a declaration was made, then there was nothing else to be done, no one to follow such a case unless one was only calling for his own death. Hundreds crowded at the site. Whoever had a missing relative declared him dead and among the bones.'

'And so I was declared dead, and among the bones.'

'Yes.'

Kato is aware that it wasn't unheard of during Obote II's regime for people to disappear mysteriously and forever. The rowdy army engaged in all sorts of deadly activities. Everyone was left to wonder who gave orders to kill who, or to capture who, or to loot whose house, or to torture who.

'Your father did his best to search everywhere for you.'

'My father didn't search enough. He never went to check with the prisons.'

'He searched. We all searched, until after the bones, when

everyone lost hope.'

'Did Edna lose hope too?'

Mzee laughs, for the first time since Kato had entered his house. 'Edna is the only person who never accepted your assumed death. She always said you would come back.'

Kato sits up straight. He smiles, and then laughs too. 'I knew she was alive too. I believed she had survived the deadly experience.' He reaches for the plate and devours the pieces of cassava. Later he puts the empty plate aside and instead reaches for the cup and gulps down the water. The water flows to his stomach then rises again to settle below his heart like a supporting cushion. He loves this feeling. Edna is alive.

'Where is she now?' he later asks.

Mzee's face is already re-arranged. The wrinkles are more pronounced now, eyes narrowed as if he is squinting. Kato can clearly tell the smile on Mzee's face has transformed into sadness.

'It wasn't only the change of government. Many things changed too. Children were born, children grew up, people died ... people ... got married—'

Kato kneels in front of Mzee. 'Are you saying Edna got married?'

Silence again. This time it's hot, blazing, drying up the water which had settled below his heart. He trembles. His body heats up. Sweat breaks through his skin. His breath quickens.

'Edna waited till she could wait no more,' Mzee finally says. 'Her wedding is pending.'

Kato pats his ears. What Mzee has just said is the loudest phrase he's ever heard yet he isn't sure he's heard it. It has to be repeated before he can believe it but he is not sure he wants to hear it again. He prefers death. He prefers being kidnapped and put in prison: locked up forever. Deafness is better so that he can never hear again. Edna. Her wedding is pending!

'Pending,' he says. 'Ten years...' for ten years he managed to convince his heart that Edna was alive, and that she was waiting for him. Perhaps it was just a means of facing life inside the high walls; living the life of a yokeless shell. It was a means of waking up every morning, toiling on the *shambas* under the blazing sun, swallowing the once-a-day meal of *posho* and beans – trying to fill the forever space in his stomach. It was the reason he was named 'escapee' and it was the reason for a successful escape. But her wedding is pending!

He extends his leg forward to expose a deep scar on the left calf. 'This is one of the marks of my trials for escape. The rest are on my chest and back. I tried, Mzee, I did the best I could, all for Edna.'

'She has tried, too.'

'Tried what?' Kato shouts.

'She had vowed to stay in her house with her son and wait for you. For seven years, she waited, and she was determined to wait, but your relatives forced her to vacate the land.'

'But it's my land, my wife's land, my son's land!'

'You were not here to explain that to them.'

'I know.'

'They harvested all the food Edna had grown, harvested all the coffee, and left the land uncultivated.'

Kato lowers his voice. 'I saw my desolate home already, Mzee. When is her wedding?'

Mzee pats Kato's arm, making skin contact for the first time. 'I wish I could tell you otherwise but…her wedding is two days from now.'

'I am not too late, Mzee.' Kato jumps to his feet. 'Where is she? I must be on my way now.'

'It's way past midnight, too late to move.'

'Things changed, Mzee. No curfews. No rowdy army. There is freedom of everything. For many years I waited to see 'the best' in the new government. Now is my time.'

'I promise you, Kato, I can only give you her home address in the morning. For now, I will make you a bed. You need some rest.'

Kato slowly lowers himself back onto the floor. He cries.

*

The face that first appears in the doorway is old and crinkled. The owner of the face is holding a hoe. Edna's mother. She stares at him, mouth agape. The hoe in her hands drops. Another face emerges from the kitchen. Edna's young sister. She is winnowing a basket of fried groundnuts. The basket drops the moment she sets eyes on him. She shouts, 'Ghost. Kato's ghost!'

More faces appear. More voices chorus, 'Kato's ghost! Kato's ghost!' Among the faces that appear there is a boy of about ten years – if he guesses. No mistake; his son! The boy dashes to cling to his grandmother's skirt. His son: the child he had never seen. The child has Edna's round face. 'My son, I am your father,' Kato whispers. He wants to rush forward and pick up his son but his body can barely move. Another face appears. It's not Edna. It is Edna's aunt. They have all gathered for the wedding. This is how they gathered when he was marrying Edna. More and more people swarm into the compound.

Edna appears. Instead of coming from inside the house taking delicate steps, her face shining with effects of *Samona* jelly; just as it is expected of any ripe bride; she emerges from a small path behind the house, a jerrycan of water balanced on her head with skill. Unlike all the people who have dropped whatever they had in their hands because of the shock of seeing him, Edna drops her jerrycan only to be able to run to him with arms opened wide. Edna. The round face. The soft, welcoming torso. He feels the warmth of her embrace. She smiles: the smile that mends the crack in his heart, the smile that drowns the darkness he's dwelt in for ten years. Edna, his bride, his wife; the mother of his son. His tears dissolve in her *kitenge*. Her tears dissolve in Mzee's shirt. He holds her in an everlasting embrace. He will never let her go. She lifts her beautiful teary, face and looks in his eyes. She says, 'There is only one thing I want to do now. I want to tell the whole world that my proposed wedding is cancelled. My husband is back!'

*

Kato rises from the unknown depths of his sleep. Mzee is holding a cold compress over his forehead.

'You were dreaming,' Mzee says. 'From what I observed, your dream had a bad beginning, but the ending brought a big smile to your face.'

'Edna still loves me.'

THE NAKED EXCELLENCIES
Yusuf Serunkuma

Most of the ministers started to arrive a few minutes after the President entered the hotel. This was not the usual arrival protocol, but rules had changed owing to the fact that His Excellency had lost trust in most of his followers and, most surprisingly, his security men, too. He had survived three assassination attempts in three years. Subsequent investigations indicated that these unsuccessful attempts were from people around him. Of course many lead suspected hit men were in jails, so events had started changing in very significant, and often, impromptu ways. Today, as it had been arranged, His Excellency arrived first — the usual thing had been arriving last and sometimes arriving late, or not arriving at all — then the arrival of ministers and later the honourable members of parliament. In a secret meeting with the Presidential Guard Group, His Excellency had said to his largely semi-illiterate guards, most of them distant and near relatives and in-laws 'Make sure the Honourable visitors are stripped of anything — no weapon, no nothing. It is a standing order.'

The first minister to arrive was a strong loyalist to the President. When told that the President had said honourables were expected to enter 'stripped of anything', he quickly threw off his jacket, undid his tie, unbuttoned the shirt and did the same with his trousers. He threw them to the ground saying;

'I have thought about that for sometime'. He had once worked as a professor of philosophy at the University of Old Kampala and was now a respected philosopher of the government. When he threw his trousers off, the Guard Group was taken by surprise. In fact a few of them giggled at the development. But on quick recollection and cunningness, they only advised him to remain at least with his undies on! And so he didn't remove everything else. He did however, grumble under his breath, blaming the disloyal members for making them suffer old age shame. To the Presidential Guard Group, this was to become the code of the day.

A few minutes after this incident, the parking spaces started to fill with the heavy chauffeur-driven vehicles with red plates. Ministers were arriving. No one protested taking off either his trousers or the jacket. The Guard Group comprised of new faces every day and new rules; ministers had become used to changes.

All the male ministers, having arrived first, obeyed the new security measures without much ado. We awaited the arrival of the female honourables in anticipation of their refusal to comply. The first female minister to arrive had been a little hesitant when asked to obey the new security arrangement, but looking at the pile of brand new and designer suits in the corner, and fearing being branded an accomplice in one of the failed attempts on the life of the President, yanked off her *busuti* and with ecstatic feet joined the colleagues on state duty. She was an old woman who in fact had little worries about shame. Her clothes were used as specimens to convince or to illustrate to the other female ministers who arrived later — there was just no space nor time for persuasion.

Soon, the conference hall was filled by naked honourables and naked ministers. It was quite risky walking away in refusal to strip; you would be considered disloyal to the Guard Group and to the President, by extension. You would definitely be haunted by your decision and would live to hate it. And no one dared court such a suspicion.

It was culture here for people to arrive past the time of the official start of events. As the meeting moved, a naked female minister or honourable would enter; her jelly belly and bulky bottom only kept in position by tight underwear or a thong passing through the ending of the spinal cord at the lower end of the back, and another running around her waist. The bottoms of most female ministers were big enough to swallow any factory made underwear — most of them thongs of course — that had been in vogue those days. Indeed, many of them appeared as if they were naked. It was just the heart-shaped fabric that stood so candidly in front of them, just below the tummies that showed they were a bit dressed. Many looked awed by this security practice and most of them were uneasy at the start of the meeting. Later it was to become old news and commonplace as all looked like they were in uniform: But for how long?

Earlier, when the first honourable — the former university professor entered the conference hall, the President cringed a bit, and was on the verge of stopping him when it suddenly occurred to him that a naked man was easier to watch than a clothed one. He let him enter that way and, he was appreciative of the Guard Group for their decision. In order not to look different, he removed his shirt, remained in his vest and sent for a quick pair of trunks. But when the female MPs entered the air changed.

Those days, MPs had money and simply bulged with wealth. They drove heavy vehicles as a marker of wealth and authority. But also, almost all ministers suffered from 'good health' — so it was called in some stubborn or just bold local tabloids. Many people in high offices often died looking supple and young, the harsh living conditions common in Africa notwithstanding. The women on the other hand had exceedingly huge bodies often tantalizing to colleagues on state duty. Fat and sexy, you know. There were less publicised, very confidential, but 'declassified' reports that male ministers made love with other female ministers despite being the wives of other men and they being husbands to some women in their homes. A story had run for six full months of one honourable who had paid off a local citizen to have his wife for himself. The wife was a member of parliament. Sometimes, it was gossiped that there existed an unwritten treaty of interchange. The wife 'exchange' dinner — as journalists in *The Green Daily*, a tabloid of some sort, coined the words. It was a common practice in symposia and in residential workshops. We would never run these stories at *Uhuru Weekly,* partly for credibility reasons, but largely for security. Yes, security; such stories attracted sales, and as the saying goes the led are never different from the leaders; as the leaders loved the acts, those led loved reading it and a daily paper would make a lot of money if it ran stories of this type. And for the tabloids that dared like *The Green Daily,* the staff lived like fugitives. But truth be told, male ministers exchanged wives — 'for internal relations sake between ministries and constituencies' so went the joke, or for 'just a night in a colleague's apartment.'

For the conference today, the female ministers were entering naked for His Excellency's security. They all sat in silence except for the clacking of heels from most of the female honourables in that endless stream of latecomers. We were accustomed to seeing them walk about endlessly at such meetings. Were they announcing the arrival of new suits like those girls lined on the catwalk trail? That we may never know. But maybe the President was right; a naked man was easy to manage. We could never believe the amount of silence and respect this meeting was accorded.

The conference neared the start but before it could fully begin, the Guard Group lashed out at us journalists and confiscated all our cameras, deleted any pictures we'd taken and then promised to return them to us after the meeting. None of the journalists were naked since they had arrived early and the head of state had little or no problem with them. Most of my friends in the job were chaps who had just left school; they posed little security threat. But none I'm sure, did his or her job comfortably in the first thirty minutes. I certainly didn't. We all looked in pleasant shock as the room turned from conference to something indescribable. The meeting started:

'...of course some of you are wondering why we are dressed like this. Why we have taken away the cameras of these watchful young boys. It is not so much for trouble. It is for our security. It is for the security of your Excellency. I do this essentially for you and your country, so let us settle and start our discussion. I know some of you are not happy with this and you are wishing thunder struck me dead but we have a saying… 'when you see a buffalo and say, 'I wish it broke its leg', that does not necessarily break the leg of the buffalo.' The honourables guffawed at the saying and some chanted the Presidential slogan 'Number One'.

'At least, we are sure; our security is guaranteed very well when we all look the same. We are all the same when we return to the way God created us'. His Excellency added. Just like a headmaster in a weekly teachers' meeting, the President doubled as Master of Ceremonies and as Chair of the meeting.

The ministers kept clapping and giggling every time the President threw a joke at them. Sometimes it was like men in church before a passionate pastor or at *Labonita*'s Thursday Comedy Night. 'Among other issues we are here to discuss.' The President continued. '…we want development for all, rural electrification, peace and security and protection of the position of the presidency. This I think, is the most important thing for today and should become number one on this agenda. It is rather absurd that the President's life is constantly under threat…I am also interested in the Business Awards that were held last week. I have learnt that you…do we have the fellow who organised the event here in the hotel?'

A fellow stood up. He was at the back of this expansive and swanky hall, in black undies, his chest was remarkably hairy. He couldn't really stand properly; it was a bit embarrassing to stand with a protruding underpants-front. He seemed to have developed that spontaneous erection which takes over just at the sight of a stripper. His name was Ssebbi Sunday. His belly stretched upfront and folded downwards hiding the front of his under cloth. He was neither a minister, nor an MP nor a member of the First Family. He had attended the meeting because of the recent addition to the constitution of the country. The recent addition required that prominent businessmen had to attend all ministerial meetings — they were expected to be friendly with the government which not only awarded them with lucrative tenders, but provided them with peace and space to go about their business.

Two weeks before, Mr Ssebbi Sunday had organised the Business Awards of the year. Public events like this attracted huge crowds and equally huge sums of money and the organisers became rich overnight. Becoming rich meant that one had to immediately join the club of men and women in the other equally rewarding economic activity; politics. All the rich had to join the ruling group. Because it was highly priced, the Business Awards had attracted a selective audience of money-men from around the country. Members of parliament had attended; ambassadors NGO bosses, and members of state cabinet were in the audience too. Businesses ranging from breweries to crafts and factory work competed for these awards. Some of the least expected but most attractive businesses although unlucky on the night went before the panel of judges too. Added to the long list of gifted local artistes for the entertainment of the guests and business men, small, five minutes exhibitions were organised for the audience and judges to fully augment their anecdotes and statistics before they could announce the most money-earning business. This involved short but dramatic presentations of what the company dealt in, how it earned its market, its marketing potential on any new innovation in the field and just like before announcing the best world footballer of a year, pictures of his great skill are played on large screens. Here people acted out their businesses. *X-Bike Brokers (XBB)* was the favourite for the most lucrative prize. It had arrived as the people's darling having invested in a motorcycle taxi business that readily picked the market and spread the entire country like a bush fire on a sunny and windy day. Public transport had been messed a great deal and so it emerged as a redeemer. The company owned close to two million motorcycles all across the country of a population that was slightly above 20 million. Almost every village had an *XBB* branded motorcycle shuttling people from one place to another; citizen transport was perceived profitable, if organised well. At least it looked to be working out for *XBB*. But *Female-Real Estate Ltd* had them outdone with fireworks of vigorously rendered and well-rehearsed strip tease displays. Their five minutes on the stage dripped with sexual fantasy; the strippers gyrated so tantalisingly, attracting endless streams of ululation from this smart crowd of professionals and foreign emissaries. Their Managing Director appeared on the stage to announce the most recent innovation; one that attracted a standing ovation — a website for distinguished honourables who found driving to the streets 'pretty old-school'. The website enables 'men of class' to get in touch with the night girls 'of class' in the most sophisticatedly secret way; to be delivered at the place of appointment just in time. But *Female Real* and *XBB* were both unlucky — the evaluators announced that both made little profits and were not worth the awards. They had to scramble for the second and third places. Some heavy weight company had the prize under its armpit. Whichever it was, the President was interested in its affairs.

Reports from the event indicated that the company that won the prize was greatly multi-profited. Among so many things, it had invested in, city and upcountry bus transport, small and large-scale industries, property trade, in womenswear and jewellery, organised events and parties and even political campaigns. It seemed not just to be running the economy, but owning it. *4M Ltd* was 'the leading real-estate-cloth-travel- industrial and event organiser company'. The announcer shouted in the microphone a sentence that sounded like rap. And so it took the award. But it was also reported that the MD of *4M Ltd* remained unknown. By all standards, this was a rich man, expected to be part of the *inner circle*. But why had he remained unknown? This was an issue of close interest to the President, and thus Mr. Ssebbi had to be invited.

Mr Ssebbi stood up. '...yes Mr Ssebbi,' the President said, 'I will give you some time in my speech to enable you tell us the name of the man who runs *4M Ltd*. Is that the company? Yes. We will give you some time...don't worry. He has to join us.'

Many heads had turned to look at this shrewd gentleman. Oh yes, he had made his way to the club of the 'Heavy Weights' with the current MC and Chair of the meeting as the undisputed champions.

Discussing issues of this type; theft and misuse of public or personal money; who has just gained wealth and how; who has just lost his wealth and why, what fate awaits this person etc, had become common on the cabinet agenda nowadays. It was feared that if such small issues were not managed properly the country would recede into turmoil. There was fear also that failure to manage rich men would allow them to join opposition groups and perhaps dislodge government. And for men who receded in wealth, that marked their end and this had to be agreed upon in principle and at a meeting. Money meant not just power, but intelligence.

As the meeting progressed inside the hotel, there were events of historic importance unfolding at the entrance. The First Lady arrived: I would not have known this had it not been for the young man I worked with at *Uhuru*. He had found a spectacle of naked bodies ensconced inside the hotel unbearable. I guessed this was partly because of his upbringing which included receiving the biggest part of his education at home, and also the strict religious code he held onto unquestionably. He had grown up in a well-made family that cherished religion and thus chastised stripping. If it were not for the pedantry of the Guard Group, he would have left without covering the event. Hanging about with the fully dressed Guard Group at the entrance was safer and more respectful for him. He told me of the story of the ministers who although wore very beautiful suits, had stinky shoes and socks. The entrance was suffocated he said, with that strong piercing stench of decaying foot sweat! He was still at the entrance as the First Lady arrived. She was greeted by the very conspicuous pile of suits and dresses before even the Guard Group, was able to say a word of welcome.

'…What? Clothes vendors are hawking suits around here! At the hotel…where did they pass? How about their market? Did he… Mambule, allow them? What? Can't you answer?'

No one spoke. The Guard Group feared this woman a lot. She was their mother; their tireless benefactor. It was an extended First Family that feared this benevolent mom. His son who headed this group moved forward. 'It is daddy's security, mummy. All those inside are naked. Yeah and…but you can walk in mummy, no need to strip.…'

It was taboo seeing the naked body of a kinsman or a curse if for a woman. Being that the Guard Group was headed by the First Lady's first son, the first relatives looked on like poodles at a beach. But of course, seeing the First Lady strip was the most unlikely thing – it wasn't going to happen. Not even for the sake of her husband's security.

The First Lady was an exceedingly beautiful woman. She had been selected from the Munyu ethnic group known for its beautiful damsels. This happened during the revolution that brought the current 'His Excellency' to power. It was a time when the most powerful had all practical rights to have the best or the biggest share of *anything*. As this woman walked to her seat, male honourables - their maleness emphasised by their nakedness - stared at her with that intimidating but passionate stare. After she had settled, the President and his wife seemed to exchange eye messages obviously in disagreement. They went on a bit longer and the President took long pauses in the middle of one point or another to communicate something to his dear wife. Eventually, he craned his neck to whisper a clear message to her. In this effort, the President had forgotten that a microphone had been precariously stitched onto his vest by one enthusiastic room worker. We all heard the whisper:

'Yes, Madam First Lady, we are all the same here, haven't Mambule's boys told you? Look at me. Why would you like to threaten your compatriots' security with dresses?' It was a vigorous attempt to display fairness: a thing that had to extend to even the First Lady. What was wrong with her stripping when all of the rest have? Yes, we are all equal before the President. The First Lady grudgingly walked to the back perhaps to look for something 'bearable'. But she was visibly not happy with the insistence from her husband, let alone the embarrassment. It clearly came out that the President didn't even trust the woman who laid in his bed. To the President, it had to be a completely naked meeting; no exceptions to the rule.

In those days, such meetings went with pomp and involved a lot of merrymaking. Local and popular regional artists and dramatists would come to entertain this dignified crowd. After the exchange between His Excellency and the First Lady, the visibly enraged head of state requested for the usual entertainment before His Excellency continued with his speech. *Strikers*, a local band that mixed rap and country music were the more regular entertainers for such dignified meetings. In a flash, its lead singer Juliet Joanna or passionately abbreviated as 'JJ', hit the floor. She had not disobeyed the security invention - yes, naked honourables, naked singer. She did exactly that which she was known for, and good at. She gyrated and provoked sexual intimacy as she danced. The air turned from meeting to the theatrical. The male honourables started to sweat. Their eyes reddened. They would turn this way and that way fighting to get a vantage point to satisfy their eyes on this beautiful and provocative singer. It was like a VIP re-do of the Business Award fete. Thunderous clapping greeted her as she wound up her act. The President returned to the podium. His audience was excited.

It was just after 'JJ' had retreated and the President got up again that the First Lady returned. She had watched the magical singer from the background. The President glanced at her as she took her seat. In turning to see his wife, the movement of his head directed the other honourables to see what had attracted the President. She was unnervingly beautiful and extremely sexier now that the capacious garments hiding her features had left her frame. She returned in red knickerbockers that embraced her skin so tightly, emphasising her shapes. Like a huge body tattoo. She seemed to have caught the President unawares for he appeared like someone seeing her for the very first time. He was overwhelmed. His voice disappeared. Meanwhile, for the first time, a man dashed to the rest rooms. One other followed and another and another and later the movements became more frequent. Had they been sitting on bombs? Some men went into the Ladies!.

It was a spectacle seeing all types of bodies in a race to the lavatories. Some small disruption of the meeting had happened. 'Well, whoever seems unsettled, can move and take a break.- go ahead' The President joked. The mumbling of the racers and the clacking of shoes through the aisles increased, many of the male honourables paced across the floor in quick steps. The meeting resumed when some of the men that had gone to the rest rooms returned. The President started to speak again, but this time from where he was seated. Something unusual seemed to have happened to the President's voice. It staggered unexplainably. Visibly, many honourables seemed to realise this, but many of them were in the same shape of mind and body; just like the President, they were excited.

'…among other issues, we have famine on our hands. The wars staged against me are bad. I am leading this country freely. I saw men die yesterday and I was really heartbroken. Why can't war end in this country. You, the honourables, what can we do? We have the next election coming up and we need to see that we are the most powerful party available….' The President continued in this disjointed monologue. The meeting had lasted close to an hour now. The men and women in the audience clapped when the head of state spoke about election and power. Some shouted 'Number One'.

'You shouting Number One are plotting to remove me from power.' The President lashed back. 'You are all the time claiming increases in this and that…don't you see people are dying in the country? Famine, war, AIDS, what are your jobs as honourables? You see, now you can't say the President is different, we are all naked…my wife, you, and all. This should be the beginning of equality….'

He went on like that for some time; in very articulate, but disorganised rhetoric. The Excellencies in the audience however failed to settle to their seats: There were endless movements to the washrooms but less people seemed to be returning to their seats. What was happening? Because the honourables were many, some were even waiting in the hallways. The President was confused. He called for a security officer to go and find out what was going on. The President thought it was a very dangerous development; could they be planning something against him from the toilets? But the honourables were in another world – the mix of male and female naked honourables had become too much! A very dangerous mixture indeed! The officer who had been sent returned and whispered to His Excellency. His Excellency grinned slightly and looked suggestively at his wife who was next to him. He held her by the hand and they retreated to the back of the hall. We all watched nervously as the President disappeared. The other honourables who had remained in their seats started mumbling between each other. They couldn't leave and had no clue of what was happening in the lavatories and were wondering what the President had retreated to do – what was so urgent? They sat there like hungry caterpillars trapped under the scorching sun.

'Stop. Attention.' A man clad in full military uniform emerged and announced on the microphone. 'The President is dead. A new regime is hereby declared. We have taken his wife and his son to the army headquarters...' The army officers had assassinated the President, who they said they had found making love to his wife, in that short 'public' corridor before the Presidential suite. It was the wrong place for such an act and thus The President was killed immediately. The Army Chief of Staff Col. Peter Ddumba was now in control, and was speaking loudly: 'Return the cameras to the journalists. We will now report on the new President.'

NOTES ON THE CONTRIBUTORS

Violet Barungi holds a BA degree in History with honours from Makerere University, Kampala. She is a novelist (*The Shadow and the Substance* by Lake Publishers, 1998 and *Cassandra* by FEMRITE – Uganda Women Writers Association 1999), a playwright (*Over My Dead Body* 1997 and *The Award-Winner* 2000). *Over My Dead Body* won the British Council New Playwriting Award for Africa and the Middle East in 1997, and has been published in African Women PLAYWRIGHTS anthology by the University of Illinois Press 2008. Barungi is also a short story writer with numerous contributions to various anthologies, literary journals and social magazines. Her first short story, *Kefa Kazana* was published in the *Origin East Africa* anthology edited by Professor David Cook and was broadcast on the BBC. She also writes for children and has produced 9 titles in that genre by various publishers, including Oxford University Press, Kenya, Macmillan Publishers Limited and Uganda Children Writers and Illustrators Association.

Jackee Budesta Batanda lives in Kampala, Uganda. She was awarded the Commonwealth Short Story Competition, Africa Region prize for her story, *Dance with Me*. Her short stories have been short-listed for the Macmillan Writers Prize for Africa, highly commended for the Caine Prize for African Writing, and published in numerous journals including *Wasafiri*, *Moving Worlds* and *The Edinburgh Review*. She has published *The*

Blue Marble, a children's picture book, and written a short story collection, *Everyday People*. Extracts of her novel, *Our Time of Sorrow*, have been published in St. Petersburg Review and in The Literary Review. Two of her short stories, *Dora's Turn* and *Remember Atita*, have recently been published in the Oxford Book Worm Series for Learners of English as a foreign language. Jackee has been Writer-in-Residence at Lancaster University, England, and Peace Writer at the University of San Diego, California. She has performed her work in Uganda, Kenya, UK, Russia and the USA. She is currently working on a new novel, *A Lesson in Forgetting*.

Princess Ikatekit was born in Kampala, Uganda in 1989. She attended Kampala Parents' School and Mt. St. Mary's, Namagunga for her primary and secondary school education, before leaving home to go to university in the United States. She discovered her love for writing at age 11 when a poem she wrote 'for mother' took first place in a poetry contest, and has been writing earnestly since. She contributes articles to newspapers and magazines, and has won many distinctions for her essays, short stories and poetry, including the 2007 National Book Trust of Uganda (NABOTU) Literary Award which she received for her poetry. She is currently a second-year student at St. John's University in New York majoring in Actuarial Science with a minor in Creative Writing. She insists to anyone at all who will listen that this mix of words and numbers is not odd at all.

Ulysses Chuka Kibuuka was born in Karera, Sheema in Western Uganda in 1953. He attained formal education at Bugongi and Kishenyi primary schools and joined St Peter's College, Tororo in 1971, and later H.H Aga Khan School, Masaka – he left school prematurely. He began literary reading in primary school and abridged novels like R.L Stevenson's *The Black Arrow*, H.R Haggard's

Montezuma's Daughter, and Herman Melville's *Typee*, have influenced his approach to adventure writing. Alistair MacLean and Eric Ambler – among others, have shaped his *whodunit* writing. My three published works; *For the Fairest* (1991), *Pale Souls Abroad* and *Other Tales* (2000), and *Of Saints and Scarecrows* (2001), were all conceived decades before their publication. Lacking higher education, Ulysses Chuka Kibuuka did petty trade in South-western Uganda during the General Idi Amin era. He later joined NRA guerrillas to oust the Dr Milton Obote's regime that he deemed as being very dictatorial. These days he is a civil/military-relations officer in the Ugandan armed forces, with lots of fiction aforethought.

 **Beatrice Lamwaka** is the General Secretary for the Uganda Women's Writers Association (FEMRITE) and a freelance writer with Monitor Newspaper. She is also a finalist of the PEN/Studzinski Literary Award 2009, and a fellow for the Harry Frank Guggenheim Foundation/African Institute of South Africa Young Scholars program 2009. She is the author of *Anena's Victory* one of the Fountain Junior HIV/AIDS Series, a supplementary reader in primary schools in Uganda. Her published short stories have appeared in *Gowanus Books, Women's World website, WordWrite* - FEMRITE Literary Journal, *PMS Journal, Mosaic Magazine,* as well as anthologies such *Words From a Granary, Today You will Understand, Aloud: Illuminating Creative Voices, Michael's Eyes; The War against the Ugandan Child, Painted Voices, Farming Ashes* and *New Writing from Africa 2009.* She is currently working on her first novel, *Beyond My World* and a collection of short stories, *The Garden of Mushrooms.*

Glaydah Namukasa is a midwife and a writer; a member of FEMRITE. Her first novel, *The Deadly Ambition* was published by Mallory international publishers, UK (Mar 2006) Her young adult novel, *Voice of a Dream* won the 2005/2006 Macmillan Writers Prize for Africa-Senior Prize. Her short stories have been published in anthologies in Uganda, South Africa, UK and Sweden. She was awarded the 2006 Michael and Marilee Fairbanks International Fellowship to attend the Breadloaf Writers'Conference in Ripton, Vermont, USA. In Autumn 2008 she was awarded the title of Honorary Fellow by the International Writers Program (IWP), University of Iowa, USA. She has also been a visiting writer in residence at City of Asylum Pittsburgh, USA and Ledig House International writers' residence, Hudson, New York. Currently she is working on her third novel.

Kelvin Odoobo is a short story writer who focuses on the trans-border Eastern African experience devoid of national boundaries and infused with old ethno-centric and the new trans-ethnic tendencies of his generation. A native of Busia, Uganda, he was born in 1981 in Kakamega, Kenya. He went to Kanduyi D.E.B Primary Schools in Bungoma, Kenya and later Mugumo-ini Primary School in Thika, Kenya. He returned to Uganda to Jinja College and Namilyango College for his O and A levels before obtaining a Bachelor of Science in Agriculture degree form Makerere University, Kampala in 2005. He has worked as an agronomist in Uganda and currently works in Kigali, Rwanda but has traveled to Burundi and Tanzania. In his work, he regularly interacts with small rural communities and draws from their diverse conditions of life and nature the inspiration for his writing. Writing is his hobby and 'bad habit' away from his professional pursuits through which he seeks to understand what science cannot explain about life. In November 2005, he represented Uganda at the Ford Foundation Student

Voices Project for Higher Institutions of East Africa as a selected author in Nairobi, Kenya. His unpublished story *An African-African* which explores the irony in the trans-East African experience won an honorable mention at the Pan African Literary Forum 2008 Africana Creative Non-Fiction Writing Contests.

 **Yusuf Serunkuma** was born in 1983 in Jinja, Eastern Uganda, Yusuf received his early literary education from his father before joining Main Street Primary School. He later joined Bishop Cyprian High School Kyabakadde in Mukono District and Namagabi Secondary School where he finished his Uganda Advanced Certificate of Education. He graduated in 2008 with a Bachelor of Arts Degree in Literature and English from Makerere University, Kampala. While at Makerere, he served as president of the Literature Association, where he mobilised young writers, organised interactive author-student sessions especially with established writers and held several writers' competitions. He has worked as a reporter and sub editor at *The Independent* magazine. He now works as editor at Fountain Publishers, Kampala.

About the Editor

Dr Emma Dawson works at the intersection of postcolonial literature and cultural studies, drawing on ethnographic research paradigms to conduct her fieldwork. She is the general Editor of CCCP's World Englishes Literature imprint, and in its fiction series. She is editing anthologies of short stories from Kenya, Singapore, Malaysia and India. The first of these anthologies in the World Englishes Fiction series was published in July 2009: *The Spirit Machine and Other New Short Stories From Cameroon*, followed by *Daughters of Eve and Other New Short Stories From Nigeria* in April 2010. There are seven anthologies in the collection in total. She is currently working on a monograph, *Beyond The Postcolonial: World Englishes Literature* (2011).

About the World Englishes Literature imprint

CCCP
Critical, Cultural and Communications Press

Educational Series
Our popular *Read Around* series, launched in 2008, has been specially designed for the secondary school classroom, and is closely correlated with the requirements of the UK National Curriculum in English, Key Stages 3 and 4. We are currently working on plans for a *Read Around Multicultural Britain*.

Fiction Series
This series focuses on the production of new writing in English, specifically new World Englishes fiction. Country anthologies of new writing in English feature in this series – writing which is newly sourced, edited and presented with a critical introduction. The series was launched with *'The Spirit Machine' and Other New Short Stories From Cameroon* (July 2009) and followed by *Daughters of Eve and Other New Short Stories From* Nigeria in 2010. Further volumes of short stories from Kenya, Singapore, Malaysia and India are planned for 2010/11.

Criticism Series
As new World Englishes Literature emerges, a body of critical writing grows and this series aims to capture these new critical viewpoints. For example, *Working and Writing for Tomorrow*, our *festschrift* for Professor Itala Vivan, contains critical essays on the South African poets Ingrid Jonker, Ingrid de Kok and Karen Press, on the fiction of Yvonne Vera (Zimbabwe), on Wole Soyinka and Chinua Achebe (Nigeria), and on South African novelist Zoë Wicomb's *David's Story*.